A Thug's Heartbeat:

Rocko's Street Justice

A Thug's Heartbeat:

Rocko's Street Justice

Niyah Moore

www.urbanbooks.net

Urban Books, LLC
300 Farmingdale Road, NY-Route 109
Farmingdale, NY 11735

ISBN 13: 978-1-64556-252-8
ISBN 10: 1-64556-252-2

First Trade Paperback Printing December 2021
Printed in the United States of America

10 9 8 7 6 5 4 3 2 1

Distributed by Kensington Publishing Corp.
Submit Orders to:
Customer Service
400 Hahn Road
Westminster, MD 21157-4627
Phone: 1-800-733-3000
Fax: 1-800-659-2436

Chapter 1

Rocko

"Aye, yo, Rock, let me have your soups and shit," my cellmate said.

"Go 'head. I said you could have 'em," I replied as I threw my sack of noodles and other snacks at him. "I don't need the shit no more. I'm out of here any minute."

"Lucky-ass nigga. I wish I was going home. I can't wait to get out. Thanks for looking out."

"No problem. As soon as they call my name, I'm running up outta here."

"I don't blame you. You going back to what you know when you get out or what?"

That was a question I had asked myself. I had been in the Sacramento County Jail for nine months, and I couldn't wait to get home. I had had a little over one ounce of weed on me when I was stopped for an illegal lane change, and the cop had decided to bust me for a probation violation. It was straight bullshit, because marijuana was legal in California, but he had said I had over the legal limit. With the cops riding my ass at every turn, it wasn't going to be easy.

"I gotta do what I gotta do, but my girl say she leaving me if I come back here," I replied.

"Well, you know I get out next month. I need to hit you up when I get out, if you still moving."

"Do that."

He got quiet for a few seconds before he said, "You know today is the anniversary of Greg's murder, right?"

Was that today? I usually never let that slip my mind. I was so happy about getting out that I didn't even trip off it. "Damn, man. That sure is today. Greg was my dog," I said.

"He was mine too. I hate that we had to lose him like that," Wes said as he hopped on the top bunk and lay down.

I bit down on the inside of my lip. Greg's murder had been looming over my head like a bad dream for the past couple of years. I was with him the night he was killed. The cops wanted answers, and so did the streets. Everybody loved Greg. To the cops, you were guilty by association. In the streets, anytime anyone mentioned Greg, they mentioned me. I was trying to leave that nightmare in my past.

I had other things on my mind. I had two weaknesses, money and sex, and I was aware of the kind of trouble those two had brought me. Troi wanted me to get a job and to leave hustling alone. I wanted more than anything to give that to her, but it never was the right time to get out the game.

I took the pictures of my wifey and my daughter off the wall and put them in an envelope. My daughter was three years old, and although I hadn't spent much time with her, I had thought a lot about how I hadn't been involved enough in her life. For one, my woman didn't know anything about her, and every time my mom or dad spent time with Niara, they reminded me of what I shitty father I had been.

"Cooper," the CO called. "Let's go."

I stood up. "A'ight, Wes. Keep ya head up in here."

"No doubt. You'll see me out of here soon."

"A'ight."

I walked out of the cell and followed the CO out. The other inmates showed me love with head nods and daps. I got changed into the clothes I was arrested in. Then they handed me my package and my release papers. Once I stepped outside, the feeling of freedom swept over me. My dad was waiting for me when I walked out. He was an older, grayer version of me and the only man I had ever idolized. I frowned because I was expecting to see my woman.

He read my expression and replied, "Troi couldn't get the time off work."

"It's all good. I'll see her when she gets off." I gave Pop a hug. "Good to see you, old man."

"Old man? Nigga, I'm hardly old. I would've come to see you, but you know how I feel about this place."

"I do. It's good."

I was happy to see my dad. He and my mom had divorced when I was two years old. Shortly after that, he had been sentenced to twenty years for first-degree armed robbery but had spent fifteen in Pelican Bay State Prison. He had never gone back after that.

He patted me on the back. "You got your weight up in that joint, I see."

"Off top. You know ain't shit to do up in there but read and work out."

We walked to his Cadillac, which was parked up the street.

"I know you happy to be out," he said.

"Hell yeah. I hate the fucking county jail."

"Me too. I be like, 'Send my ass to prison,'" he said and laughed.

"Dead ass."

We got into his car. As soon as his door was closed, he said, "You know Mai had the baby while you was gone?"

I sighed. I now had two kids, and neither of them belonged to the woman I wanted to marry. "I know."

"You plan on seeing your son?" Pop questioned.

No one knew I had a son except for my parents and my other baby mama. "One of these days. I gotta figure out a way to tell Troi first."

"She's going to be hot as fish grease when you do, and your ass is gonna burn. You don't play with no woman."

"I know it."

"You tell her about Niara yet?"

"Nope. Not yet."

"You really trying to keep them a secret, huh?"

"It's not like that, Pop, and I know what you're thinking. Troi is too classy for this ghetto shit. I can't let her go, because she makes me want to be better. As soon as I tell her about my babies, she's not going to want to be with me anymore."

"I hear what you're saying, but you shouldn't be the kind of nigga to be a deadbeat, either. I didn't raise you that way. I spent your childhood in prison, and I still handled mine. You would think you wouldn't be doing what you doing after you watched me do my time."

"I know. Being up in county had me thinking a lot about my kids, and about how much I missed you when you were gone. This week I'm going to see both. I promise."

"That's a good start. I like where your head is at."

Pop drove away from the curb to take me to my house.

"You going back to hustling?" he asked.

I rubbed my chin. Truth be told, some of the money I had off to the side had gone to maintaining my mortgage and paying other bills while I was away, and so I needed to stack some more. As much as I wanted to live with Troi, she wasn't ready for that. In the meantime, I had my own shit, and none of my bills were going to pay themselves.

"My peeps been moving this weed for me while I've been gone. I still got the connect in Humboldt, and I'm thinking about moving it to Texas."

"I thought you were quitting all that?" he replied.

"I need to, but you know how that goes. It's not the right time. As soon as I have enough saved to live good, then I'll quit."

"You've been talking about going legit for a while now. I think it's time. Ain't nothing in these streets but death, or you could end up going to prison."

"Pop, I know, but what do I do when hustling is all I know?"

"You know I know about that, but at some point, you gotta do better. When you off probation?"

"I got three more months, and then I'm free, free."

"That's when the real party happens," he said. "We gone have to do it big."

"Off top."

A few minutes later, Pop drove up to my crib. "All right, son. You take it easy. Hit me if you need me."

"I will. Thanks for the ride," I said as I got out of the car.

"Later."

I walked up the walkway to my front door, unlocked it, and went inside. I smiled as I looked around, because Troi had made sure it stayed dusted and clean. I went to my bedroom and placed my phone on the charger. I needed to scrub jail off my skin, so I took a shower. As soon as I was out of the shower, my phone was pinging with alert after alert. I sighed when I saw it was nobody but Mai. I should've left her young ass alone, but she had kept throwing the pussy at me, enticing me with her fine ass. After a while, it was like my curiosity had got the best of me. Now we had a baby boy. Right before I'd got locked up, she'd told me she was pregnant.

I ignored her texts and calls because I was going to deal with her later. I called Troi instead.

She answered, "Hey, baby."

"Hey, you couldn't take time off work to pick your nigga up?" I asked before biting my lower lip.

"I had an important meeting at work, so that's why I called your dad to get you. You home?"

"Yeah. Had to charge my phone. I just got out of the shower. What time you getting off?"

"I'm clocking out now."

"You coming over here?"

"Yeah. I'm on my way. You want me to bring you something to eat?"

"The only thing I want to eat right now is your pussy."

She laughed. "You know I can't wait for that."

"So, then hurry your ass up."

She ended the call, and I fell back on my bed. I took in a deep breath and exhaled. It felt so good to be home. I was anxious to see my future wife. I had done a lot of dreaming about her when I was gone. By the time I got dressed, brushed my teeth, and watched a little ESPN, Troi was pulling up in my driveway.

As soon as she got to my door, I opened it and pulled her in by her waist. I didn't hesitate to give her deep kisses on her neck, cheeks, and lips. Her skin was as smooth as honey, and she smelled just as sweet. I'd spent nine months away from her, and we had had no contact visits. My hands were full of all her juiciness, and my mouth was watering as I thought about how good she tasted.

"Damn, babes. I missed you," I said in her ear.

"I missed you too, baby." she moaned.

I took her shirt off and proceeded to remove her bra between kisses. We made a trail to my bedroom with our clothes.

For two hours, we made love, and afterward, we went to my favorite barbecue spot to eat. We enjoyed one another as we talked and ate. When we got back to my place, she pulled weed and swishers from her purse. She rolled a blunt, and we smoked in the living room. I put on an Amazon Prime movie, and we snuggled. The sun set before I knew it.

"You spending the night?" I asked.

"Yeah. I don't want to leave you yet."

"You should just quit playing and move in."

"I told you already. We're not moving in together until we're married, and then we gotta get that condo I want in Elk Grove."

"When we get married, I'll buy you that condo, babes."

"You ready to set a date?"

"I've been ready."

My phone rang. I reached over to the coffee table and hit IGNORE on my phone's screen because it was Mai. I knew why she was calling. She wanted to see if I was ready to see my son. I wasn't ready, and I was going to deal with her when I was ready.

"Who's that?" Troi asked.

"Business . . . I just got out, and I want to spend all my time with my baby. Business can wait." I felt bad about lying, but I needed just a few more days to work some things out.

"I thought you said you was going to stop business once you got home."

"I am, but it takes time. I gotta make sure I have enough dough to live off."

"Well, as long as you don't go back to jail, I'm good. I know you be about your money, so why should I complain? I know your heart," she said before she kissed my lips.

"Why you saying that? You want a new bag or something?"

She laughed. "Don't say it like that. Well, I did see this new Tory Burch bag and matching sandals."

"Is that right?"

"Yeah. I think I need a gift for holding you down while you were away."

I nodded. "I got you. I'll take you to get it tomorrow."

She kissed my cheek.

I lit another blunt. After the movie, we made our way back to the bed to go to sleep. She had to get up early for work, so I didn't press her for another round of sex.

Close to midnight, my cell vibrated on the nightstand, jarring me awake. I grabbed the phone, and my eyelashes fluttered as I struggled to see who was calling. It was Mai again. I dropped the phone next to me, rolled over, and moved my leg out from under the sheet. The phone vibrated again, but I didn't move.

"Rocko? Aren't you going to answer your phone?" Troi asked.

I didn't answer.

She sighed, reached over me, and snatched my phone. "Hello?"

I couldn't act like I was worried, as I was conjuring up a lie to tell her.

Mai didn't say anything before she hung up on Troi.

"Rocko? I know you're awake," Troi said.

"What?" I groaned.

"Who's calling you at this time of night from an unsaved number?"

"Probably someone with the wrong number. Everybody I know is saved on my phone. Go back to sleep."

My phone vibrated again, and Troi answered with more authority. "Hello?"

"Get Rocko," Mai said. I could hear her through the phone.

"Who is this?" Troi quizzed.

"Mai."

"Who?" Troi asked.

"Mai!"

"I don't know no My."

"Girl, you don't need to know me. Put my baby daddy on the phone right now."

"You must have the wrong number, because my man don't have no babies."

"He must not be your man, because you don't know shit. He's my baby daddy. Now, put him on the phone, bitch," Mai growled.

Troi dropped the phone on my chest. "Rocko, your *baby mama* is on the phone."

I pressed END on the screen, powered off the phone, and tucked it underneath my pillow. My heart was racing all the while. What could I say? I couldn't think fast enough. Though this would've been the perfect time to come clean, I couldn't bring myself to do it.

"Who's Mai?" Troi asked as her chest started rising and falling.

"I don't know. Go back to sleep," was all I could say.

"Did you get one of these hoes pregnant again?"

"*Again*? You're funny." I tossed the pillow over my head with a chuckle.

I was trying to play this cool. The only thing I knew how to do was lie my way out of a situation like this. This wasn't the way I wanted to come clean with her.

She punched the pillow and didn't care if my face was underneath it.

I removed the pillow from my face and stared up at her as if she was crazy. "Hey, you need to chill. I'm trying to get some rest."

"Fuck your rest. Why are you always doing this to me?"

"I'm not always doing anything to you." I fluffed the pillow and rested my head on it.

She snatched it and hit me in the face with it, as if we were going to have a pillow fight.

I snatched it from her. "Quit playing, Troi."

"I'm not playing with you, Rocko. I have no problem ending this right here, right now if you don't start talking."

I grunted but refused to speak about it.

"What about all that shit you talked about being honest and up front about everything once you got out of jail? You spent nine months away from me, and this is how you do me? Was she coming to see you?"

"Hell no!" I exclaimed.

"Liar! You want to marry me, yet you don't like telling me what you really be out here doing. If you got somebody pregnant, just keep it real."

"I didn't get anybody pregnant. Somebody is playing on my phone."

"And you don't know why they're playing on your phone? You really think I'm stupid, huh? I'm so done with your ass."

She scooted away from me and pulled the sheet in order to drape more of it over herself.

I was pissed that Mai would say all that to Troi. Troi was the only woman I wanted, and Mai knew that.

I said a silent prayer to myself. I was going to have to fix this fast.

I fell asleep again, and when I awoke in the morning, I discovered, to my surprise, that Troi hadn't left. I got up and showered. Troi did the same. She didn't bring up Mai, and neither did I. Actually, we barely said good morning to one another; it was almost as if we were afraid to start another argument.

I kissed Troi on her way out the door.

"Have a good day at work, babes," I said.

"Thanks. You have a good one as well."

I watched her get in her car and leave. I grabbed my keys and went to the garage to get into my car. It was time for me to face my issue and set things straight with Mai.

Chapter 2

Troi

Unnoticed, I followed Rocko in the black convertible BMW 625i he had bought me for my birthday a few years ago. He thought I was on my way to work, but I wasn't about to let him off the hook that easily. As I followed him, leaving a block between us, I called into work and said I was sick. I followed Rocko until he pulled his white Range Rover next to a curb on San Jose Way. I parked down the street and surveyed the area. This was unfamiliar territory, and he had never mentioned that he had any dealings in Oak Park.

He got out of the truck and walked with a strut, wearing a crisp white T-shirt, faded baggy blue jeans, and all-white Nike Air Force 1s on his size-thirteen feet. The gold chain around his neck gleamed in the sun. He walked toward a small pale green house. He flung open the worn-out gate to the whitewashed fence that surrounded the front yard as if he owned the place.

I sucked my teeth while frowning intensely. Since Rocko never disclosed information about his little street pharmacist operations, I never knew what was going on half the time. I saw only the money and material things.

I didn't want to assume anything yet, but I had a funny feeling that this Mai chick hadn't lied when I'd answered his phone.

I tapped on the steering wheel and shut the car off. I wanted to sprint to the door of that small house, but I needed to be patient and wait it out in case he was handling business. I wasn't about to blow my cover and start another pointless fight over his infidelities, especially if I didn't have any concrete evidence. But what would be the point of my great stakeout if I couldn't catch him with another woman? Rocko needed to be caught red-handed for me to accuse him rightfully of cheating. Even if I did catch him, however, Rocko was going to spew a ton of lies before even halfway confessing.

After about twenty minutes of sitting, waiting, and seeing nothing but swaying trees in the breeze, I started thinking, *Why am I even here*? Rocko could be conducting a transaction, which meant my paranoia was out of hand.

But when I started up the car to leave, a young woman came outside, and he was behind her. I shut the car off as my insides jumbled around. God, I hated to be right about him sneaking around behind my back, but the truth was in my face *again*. The core of my stomach despised me for the discovery, and my whole body started aching terribly. I felt nearly numb.

He shouted a few obscene, angry words at her. I rolled down my window, but I couldn't really hear them. The only word that I could make out was *bitch* a few times. She said something back, rolling her neck and throwing her hands in his face. He pushed her away, warning her not to do it again. She folded her arms across her chest, looking frustrated and fed up. Then she walked into the house with a natural sway of her ass. My soul became scorched from a jealous rage, but I didn't move.

The lying bastard got into his car and drove toward the other end of the street, and she came outside once again, pushing a stroller with a baby inside it.

I placed my polarized Chanel sunglasses over my eyes as she made her way down the street, walking as if she were the finest bitch in the world. My upper lip curled as disgust filled me.

I didn't think about what I was going to do as I started up my car, moved forward, and parked right in front of her house. She didn't bother to look behind her. I got out and threw my Louis Vuitton bag over my shoulder. She was already a little way down the street, heading in the direction in which Rocko had driven off. I followed her on foot. My heart pounded as loudly as my heels clicked against the concrete. While trailing behind her, I didn't know what I would say or do once I caught up to her, but I knew this meeting was long overdue. I hadn't spent the past three years being faithful to Rocko while he was in and out of jail for him to do me this way.

I took note of her shorts and halter top, which revealed her tight little tummy, one that showed no apparent signs of childbirth. Her baby-looking face told me that she wasn't old enough to drink alcohol.

It was hot outside, more than one hundred degrees, and sweat had formed between my breasts. I wanted to get back in my car and blast the AC, but my fueled anger prohibited me from doing so. Where the hell was she going, anyway?

As soon as I thought about turning around, she reached a shopping plaza and went inside a nail shop.

Cool. I could stand to get a fill, I thought as I followed behind her.

As she took a seat at a station, a miniature Vietnamese woman asked me, "Can I help you?"

"Yeah, I need a fill."

"Okay. You have an appointment?"

"No. Do you take walk-ins?" I questioned, removing my shades.

"Yeah. Sit right here, honey. I do for you."

She sat me right next to the tramp.

I put the sunglasses in my purse and tilted my head to steal a sneak peek inside the open stroller. The sleeping baby's resemblance to Rocko was breathtaking, even with his eyes closed.

My stomach twisted into more knots.

"You getting a gel manicure, Mai?" a Korean woman asked the tramp.

"Yeah, you know what I want, Cindy," she said in the same rough, raspy voice that had cursed me out when I answered Rocko's phone.

I looked over at her. She was beautiful up close, which didn't surprise me, but she was too gorgeous for her own good, much like an aspiring model from the hood. Her complexion looked smooth like sweet dark chocolate. Her long, perfectly straight virgin hair bundles flowed down her back, and the tiny nose piercing was surprisingly attractive. I instantly wondered if Rocko was taking care of her.

"Cindy, can you please cut these nails down some? I have this cute little baby, and I don't want to scratch his gorgeous face," Mai said.

Cindy nodded and replied, "Oh? You like a shorter nail?"

"I need them cut down a little bit."

"Your baby is precious," I said, keeping my eyes on the stroller.

"Thanks," Mai responded, giving me a side-eye look. She was overprotective of her son, her precious jewel. He was her only way of holding on to the man who didn't claim him as his own.

"He's really adorable. What's his name?"

She replied proudly, "Rocko Prince Cooper, Jr."

My breath escaped me like the air in an old worn-out tire with a slow leak, but I didn't show it. She had had the nerve to name her baby after *my* man.

"He's so small. How old is he?" I said.

"He's two months old today."

Two months old? She was pregnant the entire time he was locked up. Three long and painful years with Rocko, and my heart felt like it was about to burst yet again.

"Wow. It's so amazing how you mothers do it. I mean, I can't even take care of my man, let alone a child. Are you and the father together?"

She frowned and chuckled. "Together? Please, who does that anymore?"

"Well, he's such a cutie-pie."

That was the truth. Her baby really was adorable.

She rubbed her glossed lips together and stared down at her son. She shifted uncomfortably, as if she didn't like the spotlight, but I was going to keep that bright light shining on her.

"Thank you," she finally said.

"You're welcome. I don't mean to be all in your business or anything, but how involved is the father? I don't know many men who step up to the plate these days."

"I mean, it is what it is. He just got out of jail yesterday, and he saw our son for the first time today," she replied, with disappointment in her voice. "He ain't perfect, but I don't care. He can do whatever he wants."

"He can do whatever he wants? But y'all are together, right?"

She stared at me hard, refusing to answer. She wasn't going to blab her whole situation to some random stranger.

I cleared my throat as I looked around the shop and wondered what else to say to her to get her to tell me something else without offending her.

"Girl, my man . . ." I paused to think about how I wanted to come at her. "My man had a baby with another woman, and I found out today."

She examined me, looking me up and down from head to toe. "Are you serious?"

"I'm dead serious. There's only so much a woman can take, you know. You can't teach an old dog new tricks no matter how much you try. Well, at least, not in my experience."

She looked as if she was thinking about it. I could see hurt and pain behind her eyes. She wasn't happy with the fact that she wasn't Rocko's only one. She might've been in love with him, but he wasn't in love with her.

"My baby daddy also has a three-year-old daughter with someone he was with a long time ago, and she lives in San Francisco," she revealed.

Did she just say he had a baby in San Francisco? He had told me that the baby wasn't his. *Lies, lies, and more lies. Damn me for being so blind.* I fought the tears that threatened to appear.

"Wow. He sounds just as trifling as my man."

"Girl, that ain't even the half of it. Now he's talking about getting married to that plain . . . Ugh, don't get me started."

"He got a woman?" I asked, as if I didn't know, playing off how mad I was getting.

"They were together before I met him, so it's kind of like I knew before I got knocked up."

"Damn. Have you met her before?"

She rolled her neck. "No, but I hear she's some fat, light-skinned bitch."

I wasn't fat. At least, I didn't think so. I mean, I had a few extra pounds on my frame, but Rocko loved every inch of me. It was funny to hear her talk that way about me when I was staring her in the face. My ears were burning from the information she fed me. I couldn't believe she was happy with being a side bitch, and I couldn't believe how much she knew about his other baby mama.

I wanted to hear more, but my heart couldn't take it, so I chose to let silence drape over us like a thick blanket until we both were finished getting our nails done.

"Take care of that precious baby," I said to her after I paid.

I walked out of the nail shop before Mai. My thoughts, stomach, and heart were blazing in what felt like an enormous fire. I was going to kill Rocko as soon as I saw him.

As I headed down the street toward my car, she was behind me, talking loudly on her cell phone about Rocko to one of her friends, of course, and all I could do was smirk.

"Yeah, girl, Rocko is out of jail. He finally saw Junior. Mm-hmm. He gave me some more money. I'm about to catch the bus later to Arden Fair Mall."

As soon as I reached my car, right in front of her house, I thought to myself that I had to be crazy for parking there when she knew what my car looked like. When I had parked there, I had wanted a confrontation to prove she meant nothing to him, but while sitting with her in the nail shop, I had discovered she wasn't worth it. And I didn't have the time to fight for a man who was a piece of shit.

I unlocked the door with the fob on my key chain and walked quickly to get in.

She said to the person on the phone, "Girl, let me call you right back." She threw the cell phone in her purse and wheeled the stroller onto the front lawn. Pointing her finger at me, she exclaimed, "Ah, hell nah, bitch! You played me."

"Look, I don't want to start no shit with you."

"Clearly, you do."

I rolled my eyes. "Ain't nobody got time for you."

"You parked in front of my house like you wanted to see me about something, and then you followed me to the nail shop? Bitch, what's up? I'm right here. What you wanna do?"

"I don't want to do anything. You talked all that shit when I answered his phone, so I had to come see your baby for myself. You thought that baby was going to make him leave me, huh?"

The frown on her face indicated I had struck a nerve. "If you would've been handling your business like a real bitch, Rocko wouldn't have been calling me to give him some pussy and head. You got some fucking nerve to park in front of my house, jealous-ass bitch."

"And why would I be jealous of you?" I laughed hysterically. "I have a job and a college degree, honey. I can do fine without him. Can you?"

She charged at me and struck me on the right side of my face with the palm of her flat, open hand. I stepped back and stared at her as if she had lost her mind. She leaped at me again and punched me twice.

I was not about to get my ass whupped by some young little tramp. I might've grown up in the suburbs, but I wasn't a punk. Even though I had on work clothes, I turned around quickly, grabbed her by her head, and rammed it up against the hood of my car as hard as I could a few times. Her nose bled, and the blood trickled to her top lip before making a trail down her chin. She struggled to get out of my reach and landed hard on the curb.

"Do you still want to attack me?" I asked, standing over her. "Yeah, that's right. I got hands, bitch. I wasn't even trying to go there with you, but you wanted it."

She stared up at me, with a look of shock and terror combined. Her baby started crying, so she got up quickly, wiping her nose with the back of her hand.

Reaching for a baby wipe in her diaper bag, she threatened, "The next time I see you, I'ma kick ya ass."

"Trust me, boo, there won't be a next time. You can have Rocko. I'm done."

I got into my car, slammed my own door, and drove off. I stared at my shaking hands after I came to a screeching halt at the corner. I had broken a nail in half, and it was bleeding. Placing my index finger in my mouth, I sucked the bit of blood between the cracks in my nail. It started to burn instantly.

"Ouch!" I yelped.

A car honked behind me so I would go. I drove home. As soon as I was in the house, I noticed a few drops of blood on the front of my white blouse. I took off my clothes quickly, took a bath, and got in the bed. Before long I dozed off. When I woke up from my nap, I checked my phone.

Rocko hadn't called.

I got out of bed and wandered into the kitchen. As I poured myself a shot of Bacardi rum, I wondered if she had got to him. I was sure by then he had already heard about what happened, and I bet he was more than pissed off and ready to give me a grand story to persuade my deceived heart.

Night came quickly, and still, I refused to call the two-timing bastard. I wanted to save my voice for the screaming match we were going to have when he finally decided to show his face. I drank straight from the Bacardi bottle and blasted Mary J.'s "Not Gon' Cry" on repeat. I listened to it all night on full blast, singing and crying with Mary. Why was I contradicting the song? My silly tears wouldn't stop pouring as the words "I'm not gon' shed no tears" flew out of my mouth.

I plopped down in the middle of my living room and stared at my beautiful engagement ring, which was engraved with our initials. He had proposed after two years of dating. Before I'd said yes, my heart had wanted to believe that he would do right by me. Rocko was charming and handsome, and often he made me feel like a delicate flower. I had always thought that if a man—no matter if he was good or bad—loved a woman enough, he would change, and that was why I had said yes. But there was no changing Rocko, and the beautiful visions I had had of our future diminished.

I turned off the music, lay on my back on the carpet, and looked up at the ceiling. Why did I allow Rocko to control me and do whatever he wanted to do? How did I become so naive? Why hadn't he called to check on me? Did he even love me anymore?

He had never gone this long without calling, and this realization made me even madder. I stood up, grabbed the Bacardi bottle, marched out of my house, and got into my car. I started the engine and drove off, and before I knew it, I was merging on Interstate 5. After taking the Meadowview exit, I turned onto Amherst and went to his house, only to find that his car wasn't in his driveway. I drove to Pop's house in Greenhaven, but I didn't see him there, either.

"Where are you?" I asked aloud, as if he could hear me. My heart started beating faster when I thought he could be at Mai's.

I headed to her place. Every light was green as I sped through each intersection on the empty streets. As soon as I turned the corner onto Mai's street, I caught sight of Rocko's Range Rover. I shook my head and placed my hands over my face as fresh tears arrived, as if my empty well had been refilled by the night's rain.

I parked the car right next to his, picked up the Bacardi bottle, which I'd placed on the passenger's seat, and fumbled with the cap. I had some difficulty twisting it off, but once I did, I took a big gulp before getting out of the car. Wavering as I stood on my feet, I tried to throw the bottle at his truck but missed. It exploded in the middle of the street.

"Fuck you, Rocko!" I shouted, looking around.

No one was out roaming the streets at this time of night, not even a crackhead or a bum. The sound of my own voice echoed in the empty streets, and it startled me. The chilly air enveloped my flesh as I stood there in a pair of shorts, a tank top, and flip-flops. Shivering a little, I climbed behind the wheel and then searched the glove box for my switchblade.

"I gave you everything!"

With the switchblade held tightly in my shaking hands, I got out of the car and stomped over to his Range Rover. I slashed his tires one at a time, ripping those suckers up. I stepped back and admired my artwork before looking around to see if anyone was watching. I spotted a brick in the grass near the sidewalk. I tried to run and get it, but somehow my feet moved ahead of my body, and I fell right on my ass. I laughed in the middle of the street for a moment, then tried to get myself together and shake off that drunken feeling, but I couldn't.

"You really fucked me over this time, didn't you? You don't know who Mai is, right? You dumb muthafucka."

I stood up, grabbed the brick, and hurled it at his windshield, shattering the glass. His alarm went off and blared loudly. Smiling with satisfaction, I jumped in my car as quickly as I could. Fear of being caught suddenly came over me. What was I going to do if he wanted to fight? I had never been in any type of combat with Rocko. Thankfully, things had never gone that far, but I didn't know what he would do when he got mad enough.

A minute later he bolted out of Mai's house with his keys in his hand, hit the alarm button to silence the loud noise, and saw his bashed windshield and ruined tires. "What the fuck, Troi?" he yelled.

Mai was behind him, and I noticed the white Steri-Strips that had been applied to close the cut above her right eye.

I lowered my car window. My upper lip curled as I uttered, "Tell *your bitch* she can have your trifling ass!"

I made the tires screech as I peeled off down the street. There was no way he could chase me with flat tires, but I kept looking in my rearview mirror, afraid that I would see his headlights.

I went home and locked myself inside.

By now Rocko was calling my phone repeatedly, but I didn't answer.

Oh, now you want to call me.

I collapsed on my bed, and my drunk ass fell asleep. When I woke up, Rocko was right there, staring down at me. I had almost forgotten the man had a key. If I were smarter, I would've gone to my homegirl Erika's house for the night.

"Are you satisfied?" he asked calmly.

The sound of his voice irritated me and made my head throb. I needed some aspirin, and I needed it quick. I went into the bathroom and rummaged through the cluttered medicine cabinet. I usually kept an extra bottle there, but for some reason, I couldn't find it among all the junk I had in there.

Rocko appeared in the bathroom doorway. "Answer me, Troi," he said, raising his voice.

I held my forehead with my left hand and kept looking for relief, refusing to answer him.

"Will you stop and answer me?"

"What, Rocko? What do you want from me?"

"Why'd you do all that shit yesterday? You had no right to follow me over there. I had to take her to the damn hospital."

"I had no right? Wow. You're something else." I took a deep breath and started looking through a vanity drawer. "And I could give a fuck about her going to the hospital. The bitch attacked me."

"Ever since we met, you've accused me of cheating."

I stopped digging in the drawer and narrowed my teary eyes at him. "Oh, so this my fault? From day one, you already had a woman, didn't you? And she was pregnant with your baby, but did you tell me that!"

He changed the subject. "You never trusted me in the first place."

"Rocko, please. You got two kids. Not one, but two, by two different women. You lied to me, and I stayed like a damned fool, but I'm not going to put up with your dirty ass any longer. I've had enough of your shit."

"I know you're hurt right now, but I can explain if you let me. I never meant to hurt you. I had to see my son today. I missed out on his birth . . . Listen, I can make everything right," he replied.

"Rocko, the only way your shit will be okay with me is if your ass disappears from my life for good. Let Mai hold you down when you go back to jail."

I found the aspirin behind a few empty prescription bottles, popped two in my mouth, got a glass, and poured some water in it. I gulped down the water so fast, I almost choked. I caught myself and swallowed the pills.

"I guess you can give back everything I bought you, then," he said, as if I cared.

"I sure can." I went into the bedroom, tossed the clothes he had bought out of my closet. I went to the jewelry box, threw bracelets on the floor, took off the engagement ring, and slammed it into the palm of his hand. "Are you happy now? Will you leave me alone now?"

"Come on, Troi. Are you going to let me explain?"

"You've had plenty of time to explain, and you blew it. You've done nothing but make my life a living hell since

I met you. I don't believe for one second that you ever loved me."

"That's not true. I love you with my whole heart."

"If this is love, then I don't want your fucked-up love."

"You really want this to be over? Is that what you're trying to tell me?"

I rushed into the bathroom and threw up my insides in the toilet.

"Babes," he said and knelt next to me.

I pushed him away. "I want you to get out of my face and step the fuck off."

"You don't mean that." He touched my hair, but I pushed him away harder.

I flushed the toilet and washed my mouth out in the sink.

His eyes softened up while he pleaded, "Don't do this, babes."

"You fucked up."

"I fucked up, but I was going to tell you about the kids when the time was right."

No, he didn't go there.

"Go take care of your kids and get the fuck out," I said as I walked into the living room, knowing he would follow me.

He tossed my house key on the coffee table. "When I walk out this door, Troi, I'm gone for good."

"Goodbye and good riddance."

Reluctantly, he walked out the front door and closed it behind him.

He was gone, but as tears welled up in my closed eyes, I couldn't help but feel as if I had lost everything. I couldn't wait to stop crying.

Chapter 3

Heather

My phone was chiming in the middle of the night. That was something that hardly ever happened unless it was an emergency. I picked up the phone and grimaced as I tried to see the number. I heaved a sigh, releasing air from my slightly parted lips, when I saw Rocko's name across the screen. Why in the hell was he calling me?

"What?" I answered angrily.

"That's how you answer the phone, Heather? You didn't answer not one letter I sent, and you didn't bring my baby girl to see me. I'm home now, and I want to see her. Come open the door."

That woke me up completely, and I sat straight up in bed. I blinked a few times, trying to make sense of why he thought it was okay to come to my house in the middle of the night.

He rang the doorbell. "It's me, Rocko," he told me on the phone.

I made a disapproving groan. "I know who it is, fool. Why are you here?"

"I want to see my daughter."

Rocko had seen her only two times in her whole life. For all she knew, my boyfriend was her daddy.

I eased out from under my warm blanket, and a cool draft greeted me. I sat on the edge of the bed, feet dangling. "I know you're not really at my front door right now."

"That's exactly where I am. Don't make me ring the doorbell again."

"Yeah, please don't do that. I don't want you to wake Niara up."

"Okay, so open the door."

I stood up and walked out of my bedroom. "You drove all the way from Sacramento in the middle of the night to see Niara? Couldn't you wait until the morning?"

"I could've, but I didn't want to wait until then. I want to see her right now."

I frowned. Everything always had to be on his timing. He was a "right now" type of man, and it was irritating as fuck.

"What do you need to see her right now for?"

"Why you acting like that? Is *he* in there or something?"

"You showed up here unannounced, so don't worry about who I got up in here."

"Are you going to let me in or what?"

I walked down the stairs slowly. My boyfriend and I didn't live together, but we had keys to one another's places.

I pulled my shorts down from where they had risen and made sure I was decent before going down the second set of stairs. After running my fingers through my short mane, I turned on the hall light and stared through the peephole in the front door. Rocko was indeed at my door, as he'd said.

I flung open the door. "What in the hell are you doing here?"

He stared at me as if he didn't recognize me. "Damn, Heather, look at you . . ."

Everything about the old me, I had to let go of. I had shed seventy pounds and had cut my hair. I was no longer the overweight, insecure girl who hid behind her long, curly hair. I was a strong, proud woman who walked with her head up.

I closed the door after I let him in. "Does Troi know you here?" I asked.

Without responding, he followed me up the stairs to the living room and sat on the couch. He made himself comfortable as his eyes drank in my body from head to toe.

I leaned up against the wall and folded my arms. "Why are you here?"

He avoided that question as he observed everything about me. "Nothing was wrong with the way you used to look, if I'm allowed to say that. How have you been?"

"Your *daughter* is fine." I rolled my eyes.

"I came by to check on you guys."

"Stop right there. Hold up." I paused as I tried to make sense of this. "You came by in the middle of the night to check on us? You could've called for that."

"True, but I'm here now, so can I go upstairs and see my daughter?"

"No. She's sleeping, like she should be. You do know she turned three last month, on the thirteenth."

He looked as if what I said didn't affect him. "Of course I know that. That's why I sent her birthday money through my mother. Did you get it?"

"Yeah, but she didn't get her daddy."

"Well, unfortunately, Daddy was doing a little time." He picked up a baby doll that was lying next to him on the couch. "Look, Heather, I don't want my only little girl to grow up without me. I know I haven't been perfect, and I need to do better. Life is too short."

I could hear Niara coming down the stairs, which upset me because I hadn't wanted him to wake her up. She walked straight to me.

I picked her up as she rubbed her eyes.

"Mommy," she whined.

"Shhh," I whispered, rubbing her back.

"She's gotten so big now." He seemed to be surprised at how much she had grown since the last time he saw her. He put the doll aside, stood, and extended his arms toward us.

"Niara," I said. "Look, sweetie. Do you know who that is?"

She stared at him as she responded, "That's my daddy."

"Yes, Niara. It's your daddy," he said.

She buried her head in my shoulder, but then she looked up at him. He reached for her again, and she slid down my waist to go to him.

He lifted her up and stared into her eyes before he hugged her. "Heather, she's so fucking pretty. She looks like my mother."

"She does," I admitted.

Niara wrapped her arms around his neck. He kissed her forehead and held her as if he never wanted to let go. Niara got comfortable in his arms as he caressed her hair.

I hated to interrupt their little reunion, but it was not the time to do this. I was ready to go back to bed. "Are you going to come back in the morning or what? Not to kick you out or anything, but we're going back to bed."

"Can I stay? I'll take her back to Sacramento with me as soon as the sun comes up."

"I'm not sure I understand why you think that's a good idea. Your woman doesn't even know about her."

He looked at me as if what I had said wasn't what he had thought I would say. "Let me crash here. I don't want to jump on the freeway to go back home, and I don't want to find a hotel this late. I can sleep right here on the couch, with Niara in my arms."

I examined his face, but I couldn't figure out why he had the sudden urge to be around her. I hoped he wasn't going to keep popping in and out of her life as he pleased, but his sincere expression was one I hadn't seen before, and it made my heart soften a little.

"As soon as the sunlight peeks through these blinds, I want you gone. I'll think about whether I want you to take Niara with you."

"All right," he answered. "That's fine."

I went to the hall closet to get him a blanket. I tossed it next to him as he sat down on the couch, Niara still in his arms.

"Thank you," he said, taking off his shoes.

I walked upstairs to my room without another word to him.

Forceful, rough hands jerked me out of my sleep. I looked up, and Jared was staring down at me with an uncomfortable and distraught look. The tiny freckles resting on the bridge of his nose had disappeared underneath the redness that had consumed his face. I stared at my window and saw that the sun was shining.

"Why is Rocko sleeping on your couch with *my* daughter on his chest?"

"Jared," I replied, sitting up. "Can I tell you what's going on before you overreact?"

His chest heaved up and down. "I'm listening."

"He came to see Niara."

Jared's light brown eyes glared at me. Jared knew Rocko. They were childhood friends, and they had been best friends at one time in their lives. When I went into early labor, the first person I called other than my mother was Jared. He came to the hospital without thinking twice about it. He hated the way Rocko treated me. Jared had always been a good friend to me. Our friendship had developed into a loving relationship, and their friendship had ended in a fistfight.

"When is he supposed to be leaving?"

"He should be getting up now," I replied. "He wants to take Niara with him to Sacramento."

His eyebrows rose to his hairline as he shouted, "Fuck, no, Heather!"

I tried to ease his anger and frustration by saying, "I know it sounds crazy, but he seems like he really wants to spend time with her today. Plus, I could use a break."

"If you want a break, send her to your mama's house."

There was a knock on the bedroom door. Jared looked at me through his narrowed eyes as if he wanted to kill me. The two of them hadn't been face-to-face in years, and the pit of my stomach turned. I didn't want these fools fighting in front of my child.

"Be cool, baby," I said to Jared in a soft voice before opening the bedroom door.

Jared huffed and puffed as he stood close to my backside.

"Is it cool that I take her with me?" Rocko asked, with Niara in his arms.

"Yeah. Let me get her things together and put them in her suitcase," I told him.

"I don't need a suitcase. She'll be fine with just a few things."

Rocko and Jared exchanged glances. Neither one of them felt the need to say anything to the other.

"I'm going to pack a bunch of her stuff, because you don't know what she needs," I said, trying to ease the tension.

Jared's five-foot-ten frame was giving off such a defensive vibe that I thought he was going to hit Rocko, and Rocko smirked at the notion.

"Come get this suitcase, Rocko." I walked across the hall to Niara's bedroom.

He followed me, but not before he could look Jared up and down.

Jared stormed down the stairs and out the front door, slamming it behind him.

"I see you two still rocking," Rocko said with a stern look on his face.

I ignored him and changed the subject. "When will you have her back?"

"I'm going to take her to see my mom and dad. We'll be back tomorrow."

"Okay. She's going to really like that. Niara loves your parents. Have you come clean with Troi about her?"

"Yeah, she knows about her now, but we broke up. She ran into Mai."

I remained silent, wondering how that had ended up happening, but then I shook it out of my head. That was none of my business. I knew about Mai only because she had gone out of her way to introduce herself at Rocko's mother's house. She wanted our children to know one another, and I didn't trip, because our children needed to know one another regardless of whether Rocko was around or not.

I tried to find Niara's cutest outfits, but I couldn't seem to see what I was looking for. Everything I wanted her to wear was dirty. I hadn't gotten around to doing the laundry yet.

"Stop. I'll buy my baby some clothes and diapers. Don't worry about it."

"First of all, she's potty trained, so you don't need diapers. She wears a 3T in clothes. Are you sure you don't need an outfit or two?"

"I got this. We'll be fine."

I looked him right in his eyes, searching for a reason to change my mind. I was so nervous about him taking my baby that I was close to changing my mind. She spent the night away from me only when she went to my mother's house.

"Heather, relax this weekend," he said, reading my mind. "Have that nigga take you to Scoma's."

Scoma's Restaurant had the freshest seafood in San Francisco, and I hadn't been there since the last time Rocko took me, which was years ago. He was always trying to throw his money around.

"Rocko, I need you to get over your feelings about Jared. You two really need to talk things out. You were raised together."

"Exactly. Our moms are still best friends and raised us like cousins. We took baths together as babies. You see where I'm coming from? He could've told me he was digging you. Now you got our baby's godfather playing like he's her real daddy. It doesn't make any sense to me. He violated the code. Why he got you and my baby in this apartment, anyway? Y'all deserve better. What you do with the money I sent you?"

"That money went into her college fund."

"Oh, that's dope and smart. I got more to put in there."

"Okay."

He looked out the window while I changed her out of her pajamas. "I have to get her car seat out of your car. Which one is it?" he said.

"That white Honda parked right in front of the door."

"That old, beat-up Honda?" Stepping away from the window, he badgered me with a scowl. "As much dope as that nigga sells, he can't buy you a new whip?"

"The only thing I ask for Jared to do is to love us. I can buy my own shit. I'm working on building my credit. I don't want to live in public housing forever."

He seemed to be thrown off by my response. He was speechless, unable to come up with a rebuttal.

I put on Niara's coat and shoes. We walked down the stairs and out into the crisp, cold bay air.

"Rocko, all I ask is that you don't get into any trouble while she's with you. I swear, if you have any warrants, you're not taking her anywhere. Wait, do you have any warrants?"

"No. I just got out of jail."

"Are you on any type of probation?"

"Yeah, but I'll be off in three months."

I grabbed the car seat out of my car. I secured the car seat in his truck and strapped Niara into it, my heart racing all the while.

"She'll probably go back to sleep during the ride," I said.

"Okay," he said. "Thank you."

"Please, call me if anything goes wrong. That's my baby, and I wouldn't know what to do if something happened to her."

"Relax. She's my baby too. I got her."

I kissed her face, wanting to take her back in the house and tell him we could do this some other time, but I stopped myself because he was her father.

"Bye, baby," I said.

"Bye, Mommy."

His eyes were soft as he said, "While I was away this time, I got to thinking about how fucked up I've been. It's time that I be a man and step up to the plate like my pop did. I had her picture up in my cell the entire time. I love my baby girl."

"How'd you get a picture of her?"

"My mother sent it."

I placed my arms across my chest and fought the uneasiness swirling in the pit of my stomach. "If you have any questions, call me."

"I will. Enjoy your weekend."

He hopped in his truck, and I headed back inside.

My cell phone started ringing, so I jogged upstairs to get it. When I looked down at the screen, I saw that it was my mother calling.

"Hi, Mom," I answered before the call could go to voicemail.

"Hey, baby. What's wrong?" she asked, as if she were a psychic.

I replied quickly, trying not to sound too troubled. "Nothing. What you doing up this early?"

"Something told me to give you a call. Is everything okay over there?"

I wasn't going to be able to hide this, so I had to tell her. "Rocko showed up here late last night. Niara left with him this morning."

She was silent for a second, and I could hear her breathing become slightly erratic. "Did you say Rocko showed up?"

"Yeah, but—"

"When he get out of jail?"

"Yesterday."

"So, you let him take our baby?" she asked in a voice that was one octave higher.

"Mama, I'm going to go back to sleep."

She grunted and sucked her teeth. "I can't believe you still trust him enough to let him take off with our baby, and you about to sleep okay, knowing that? What does Jared think about all of this?"

"Jared is pissed, but he'll get over it. What choice do I have? Rocko is her father," I replied, shifting my weight to my left leg. "I can't refuse him if he wants to be in her life. I won't do that to her. She knows he's her father."

"Because he helped make her don't make him her father, Heather."

"Mom," I groaned, rubbing the back of my neck. "I'm not in the mood for that right now."

"Well, I'll pray for him, but he really doesn't deserve anything after the way he dogged you out. You don't owe him a muthafuckin' thing."

"True, but I didn't do it for him. I did it for Niara."

"Hmm. Anyway, you and Jared should swing by later for dinner."

"That sounds good, Mama. I'll call you when we're on our way."

"Okay. Bye. I love you."

"I love you too."

"Call me the minute Rocko does anything crazy with our baby, you hear me?"

She didn't have to worry about me calling her. I would hunt Rocko down and kill him if he put her in any type of danger while she was in his care. Still, I had to keep a positive mind to have peace. "I don't think he'll do anything crazy, but I'll call you, all right?"

"Good. I'll see you later."

"I'll see you later."

I hung up, crawled into bed, looked up at the ceiling, and said a silent prayer for protection. I couldn't help it. Suddenly, all the crazy memories Rocko and I shared came crashing down on me like the waves in the sea during a tsunami.

Rocko and I got together in the ninth grade. That was when we both lived in Sunnydale projects. He was selling dope, and I thought it was cute that he had hustle about him. I used to volunteer to hold money for him, and I even hid drugs in my mama's house right before his very first bust. Rocko was my world.

On his eighteenth birthday, he caught a case and went to jail for a year. I held him down while he was away. When Rocko got out, he moved in with us because his mother didn't want him with her. I got him to go back to school, and we worked hard to get his GED.

Soon I got pregnant. We started fighting over Rocko staying out too late and disrespecting my mother's household. He got caught with more guns and more dope, so she kicked him out. He moved to Sacramento. When I was seven and a half months pregnant, he gave me a key to his new apartment, and for a while, his home was my weekend getaway. Then he started ignoring my calls, so I went to his place. When I opened the door to his apartment, Troi was sitting on his couch, wearing a black satin nightgown, with her bare feet up. She looked up at me, confusion appearing on her face. Instead of turning around and leaving, I stepped inside.

I looked around for Rocko. He wasn't in the living room or the kitchen, which was adjacent to the living room. I could hear him in the back of the apartment, talking on the phone about moving more dope.

She kept her eyes on me, waiting for me to say something. I remembered this now like it was yesterday.

"Is Rocko here?" I asked.

"Yeah, he's here, but who are you?" she questioned, standing up.

I didn't say a word as I debated with myself about whether I should explain myself to her.

"Hello? I'm talking to you. Who are you?" she said.

"Oh. My name is Heather. And you are?"

"Don't worry about who I am, Heather. Why do you have a key?"

Rocko came out of the room. When our eyes met, instant tears blurred my vision.

"What's going on, Rocko?" I asked, holding on to my protruding stomach. The baby was kicking me like crazy, and my swollen legs felt weak.

"Who's this bitch, Rocko?" she asked. "She just opened your door with a key. Is she having your baby?"

Rocko sighed heavily and looked up at the ceiling.

I hated confrontations and didn't care for drama. She was the reason why he didn't check for me anymore.

"Obviously, you and I are over," I said, dropping his key on the floor. "I'm gone for good this time."

"This time?" Troi asked. "Rocko, you better start talking."

"What you want him to say to you?" I asked, irritated. "Can't you see I'm pregnant?" I pointed to my stomach. "I have a key to his spot, and he's standing right here, looking stupid."

Rocko wouldn't make eye contact with me, so I turned and ran out the door and raced to my car.

When I got to my car, I looked behind me, and she was coming after me. Rocko came running out after us.

Then he finally found his voice. He said, "Wait, babes, I can explain. Let her leave so we can talk."

Babes? He was calling her by the nickname he had always reserved for me.

His words didn't slow her down one bit. "Wait up," she said to me. "Let's go ahead and get everything out on the table. Let's talk like grown women."

I spun around, with tears streaming down my face. "I'm due in two months, and before Rocko was your man, he was my man for four years."

Unexpectedly, she attacked me like some wild banshee. I didn't see it coming and didn't expect her to hit me while I was pregnant and knock me to the ground. I thought she wanted to have a conversation like grown women did.

Rocko managed to grab her by both of her arms and lift her away from me.

"Get your hands off me, Rocko! Get off me!" she shouted, hitting him in his chest.

"Babes, calm down. Please, calm down. This is all one big misunderstanding."

"Help me understand, Rocko! Is she having your baby or not?" Troi shouted.

"It's not mine."

I was writhing in unbearable pain while they argued with one another. He didn't seem to notice me struggling to get up. He didn't seem to care. They kept shouting back and forth. I climbed in my car and drove away, and the whole way back to the bay, I had labor pains. It got so bad that I drove myself to the hospital.

The front door opened, jolting me out of the painful memory, which had almost brought me to tears.

Jared walked up the stairs and into my bedroom. He sat on the bed.

"Are you okay?" I asked.

"I'm good now that he's gone."

"Are you sure?" I studied his light brown eyes.

"You've always been too good for him. You forgave him when you didn't need to, and you loved him when you didn't have to. I don't want him to ruin this for us. He hasn't been here for Niara like I have."

I wrapped my arms around his waist and kissed him. "I know. I appreciate everything you've done. Know that."

"How often is he coming to get her?"

"I have no idea."

He sighed heavily. "If he screws up one more time, I don't want Niara to have anything to do with him ever again."

That was something we both could agree on. "I'm with you on that."

He examined me with a weird expression on his face. "You don't still care about him, do you?"

My eyebrows sank into a deep frown. "Are you seriously asking me that question? Jared, you know firsthand that Rocko has taken me through hell and back. I will never go there again."

"Did he say anything about Troi?"

The mere mention of her name made the deep hatred I had for her curdle in my core. "He said that she knows about Niara now, and that they broke up."

I rested my head in the crook of his neck. I hoped that whatever reason Rocko had for showing up wouldn't make me regret letting him back into our lives.

Chapter 4

Mai

My son's piercing cry woke me up. I ran to him and picked him up. His skin felt extremely hot as I rocked him against my chest to quiet him. I grabbed the thermometer from the dresser and tried to put it in his mouth, but he kept moving his head. I noticed he had a white coat on his tongue from the milk he had drunk. He wouldn't be still. I tried to give him a bottle to calm him, but he didn't want it. I paced the room with him screaming in my arms.

"Wait a minute, little man. Let Mommy check your temperature."

This time I placed the thermometer under his arm and waited until it beeped. He had an elevated temperature of 101.3 degrees. My mom was one of the head nurses at UC Davis Medical Center, but she wasn't home. I grabbed my cell phone and looked at the time. It was close to midnight, so I had to call the advice nurse.

"Thank you for calling UC Davis Urgent Care Center. How may I help you?"

"Yeah . . . My baby has a high temperature, he's screaming, and he has this white gunk in his mouth that won't come off."

"Has the baby been seen here before?"

"Yes."

"May I have the baby's name?" she asked, but I could barely hear her with him making so much noise.

I did my best to shush him before I replied, "His name is Rocko Prince Cooper, Jr."

"Birth date?"

"April eighth."

"The baby has a fever?"

"Yes. It's 101.3."

"Did you try to wipe the white coat out of his mouth?"

"Yeah, and it won't come off. Looks like milk, but it's stuck."

"I need you to bring him in as soon as possible."

"Okay. Thank you."

I hung up the phone, packed the diaper bag, and called Rocko.

He didn't answer, so I left a voice message. "Look, I don't know where you're at, but Little Rocko is sick and needs to go to the urgent care center right now!"

I hung up. *Shit.* It was too late to hop on the bus, and I didn't want to walk seventeen blocks. Luckily, Rocko called right back.

"Rocko, where you at?"

"Why is my son screaming like that?"

"He has a fever, and I need a ride to the hospital."

"Where's your mom?"

"She's at work tonight."

"Can she come get you?"

"Why you so worried about her? I'm asking you to pick us up."

"I'm out of town right now. Give him some Tylenol and call it a night."

I placed my hand on my hip and shouted, "You're so fucking dumb. Are you listening to what I said? He has a fever. This is an emergency!"

He hung up the phone in my face.

No, he didn't hang up in my face.

Out of frustration, I threw my phone on the floor, and the screen shattered. "Damn it." I picked it back up to make sure it still worked. Thankfully, it did.

I had to think, because I really needed to get my son to the hospital. I wasn't going to call my best friend, Neiosha, because she was asleep at this hour. She would curse me out for waking her up.

Then it hit me. I knew exactly whom I could call. Cipher, a light-skinned cutie from around the way. And he would be up. Hustlers rarely slept. Plus, he had a little bit of a crush on me.

"Mai?" Cipher answered with a hint of shock in his deep voice.

"Hey, Cipher. What you doing?"

"I was about to go grab some Swishers from the corner store. What's popping?"

"Nothing . . . Well, I actually need a really huge favor from you."

"What kind of favor?"

"My baby is sick, and I need a ride up to UC Davis."

"Oh no, not little man. I got you. You ready now?"

"I'm ready. Are you far away?"

"Nah, actually, I'm close. Over by Fourth Ave."

"Okay. Thank you so much. I'll be outside."

"I'll be there in, like, two minutes."

I wrapped up the baby and went outside. Within minutes, Cipher was pulling up in his classic Thunderbird with the T-top.

We headed to the hospital, and after being seen in urgent care, the baby was given antibiotics for what they called thrush. Cipher waited for me in the lobby without complaining one time.

"Is he all right?" he asked when we appeared.

"He's going to be fine," I replied.

"Good. You know that you can call me anytime, right?" he said. "Matter of fact, I want to be the man in your life if you let me."

I stared at his handsome face as we walked out of the hospital. I liked the partial gold grill on his bottom teeth because it matched the golden tone of his skin. Cipher was beyond sexy to me. There had always been something about him that made me feel this magnetic attraction, but because I was trying to be loyal to Rocko, I never hollered at him.

We got into his car.

"Trust, I'll be calling to hook up with you soon," I said.

"That's cool as long as it doesn't cause any issues between you and your baby daddy. I mean, I really don't care, but I don't want him tripping out."

"Fuck him," I replied assertively.

"I feel you, Mai. You don't need him, anyway. What you need is right here. I'm the kind of man that'll take loving care of you."

"Is that right?" I licked my lips in anticipation of finding out what he meant.

He nodded his head. "You already know, Mama. All you gotta do is hit me up. It's never a problem."

Within ten minutes, he pulled up in front of my house.

"Thank you again," I said.

"Don't sweat it. Call me anytime for anything."

I climbed out and lifted the baby from the back seat. Cipher helped me by pulling the baby's seat out of the car and walking me to the door.

As soon as I got in the house, Rocko had the nerve to call me. He wasn't doing anything but pissing me off. I sent him to voicemail.

I went to William Daylor Continuation School with my mom first thing the next morning. She had always stressed how important it was for me to finish high school. She had had me when she was sixteen and had finished high school with me on her hip, so she expected me to do the same thing. I respected my mother because she had raised me alone, without a father figure. She had a longtime boyfriend, but she had never moved him in, and she had never put him before me. I was proud of her because not only was she one of the head nurses at the hospital, but she also owned our home.

"Well, Mai, you start on Monday. You ready?" my mama said as she drove us home.

"Yep." I nodded.

My mama's skin was the color of rich mocha coffee. I didn't look anything like her, which meant I could've looked like my father, but I wouldn't know, because I had never seen him, not even in pictures.

"Have you talked to Rocko about helping you with day-care expenses?"

"Yeah. He said he would."

"Good. Are you two still fighting?"

"When are we not fighting? He's always acting like a damn weirdo," I replied, shaking my head and looking out the window.

"I still can't believe he let that woman come to my house. I wish I knew where she lived. I would beat her ass my damn self for putting her hands on you."

I rolled down the window to get some air. "Look, Mama, I don't want to talk about that."

She rolled her eyes and changed the subject. "What you want to eat for dinner tonight?"

I sighed heavily. "I kind of have a taste for some steak or something."

"We need to hit up the grocery store, then."

My cell phone rang. It was Cipher.

"Hey, you," I answered quickly, excited to hear from him.

"Are you done handling your biz yet?"

"Yeah, I'm on my way home now."

"I'll meet you at your house, cool?"

"That's fine." I smiled.

"See you in a bit."

"Yeah." I hung up.

"Where you going?" Mom asked.

"Cipher wants to stop by for a little while."

"Is that his real name?"

I rolled my eyes. She wasn't big on street names. "That's what everyone calls him."

"Where did the name Cipher come from?"

"Don't know. Don't care."

"I've heard that name before. Isn't that Neiosha's man?"

I frowned. She was always up in somebody's business. "You're talking when you don't even know what you're talking about."

She shrugged. "I know he used to sleep with Neiosha. I know that 'cause y'all talk too damn loud. You want my opinion?" She didn't wait for my answer. "If that's your friend's man, you need to leave him alone."

I sucked my teeth and sighed. Cipher used to fuck around with Neiosha, but it wasn't serious now, making him available for the taking. Neiosha was playing around. She had too many niggas on her team to be worried about Cipher.

As we pulled into the driveway, Cipher pulled up behind us with perfect timing.

"Mom, can you watch the baby for a little while?" I asked as we climbed out of the car.

"You leaving with him?" she asked, taking the baby out of the car.

"Yeah, for a little while."

"Just be back in time for me to go to work tonight."

"I know. Thank you."

I walked over to Cipher's car, its twenty-two-inch rims gleaming in the sun, and he was looking the way I liked, fine as hell. He rolled down the passenger window.

I bit my lower lip to hold in my excitement as I leaned inside his car. "Hey, you."

He looked at me from head to waist, his eyes so low I could barely see them. He was digging my style as he rubbed his hands together. "Get in the car with your fine ass."

I giggled. "Let's go."

I knew what I wanted to do with Cipher, and he was down with getting freaky. Right when my hand touched the handle to open the car door, Rocko pulled up behind Cipher.

Cipher looked in his rearview mirror. "You want me to come back?"

"Nah . . . I'm about to tell him to leave."

Rocko jumped out of his Range Rover and wore a deep frown as he looked at the back of Cipher's car. Then he stomped up to me, grabbed hold of my wrist, and yanked me toward the lawn. I tried to snatch my arm away, but his grip was too tight.

I looked at him as if he had lost his mind. "Don't put your hands on me."

"What the fuck is he doing here, Mai?"

"Don't come over here trying to tell me what to do."

He squeezed my wrist tighter, hurting me. "Tell him to leave right now."

"No." I tried to twist my hand to free my arm, but once again I couldn't, because he was too strong.

"Don't fuck with me. I'll tell him to leave myself if you don't."

"What in the hell is wrong with you? Let me go!" He held me so tight, my hand was losing circulation.

At that moment Cipher got out of his car and stood there, watching.

"I thought you said my son was sick. Why aren't you in the house, taking care of him?" Rocko barked.

"You weren't so worried about your sick son last night, when I needed to take him to the hospital, so save the drama with your dramatic ass."

"I was in San Francisco, picking up my daughter. I'm here now, so shut the fuck up."

"Is she in the car?"

"Yeah."

Instant jealousy filled me as my eyes narrowed.

My mom appeared on the front porch. "Is there a problem out here?"

"No, Mama. Go back inside," I called.

Rocko released me. "I'm not feeling this bullshit. You better not leave with him."

"You're hilarious right now. He took your son to the hospital last night. Where were you at? Huh? Not here!"

"You fucking this nigga?" He raised his left eyebrow with suspicion.

I hadn't yet, but I wanted him to think I was. "Wouldn't you like to know?"

He bit the inside of his mouth. "I don't want you hanging around with him."

I put my hands on my hips and rolled my neck. "Why not? What's wrong with Cipher? You jealous?"

He stared at me for a moment, as if he wanted to say something but didn't know how to say it. He chuckled a little and shook his head. "I wish you would act a little more mature, Mai. There are things you think you know, when you have no idea. If you keep acting like a dumbass airhead, you won't see me around here anymore. I can promise you that." Anger was in his eyes as they darted from Cipher to me a few times.

"Fuck you, Rocko."

"Mai! Is everything all right out here?" my mom asked again.

"I'm fine, Mama. Go back in the house. Damn."

She walked back into the house reluctantly, but that didn't stop her from giving Rocko an evil glare first.

I looked over at Cipher, who seemed to be keeping a close eye on us.

"Get in my car so I can talk to you for a minute," Rocko said to me.

I stared him down with a smirk on my face. He didn't want me to question anything he had going on, but he wanted to be all up in my business. I wasn't in a relationship with him, so why did he care so much?

"I don't have anything to talk to you about. I have shit to do."

"Don't you dare, Mai."

"Are you done? I have somewhere I need to be . . . with Cipher."

He clenched his teeth together and balled up his fists. "Don't make me beat your ass out here, in front of everybody."

"Do it, then!" I screamed, putting my hands in the air.

He walked away toward his car, hopped in, and gave Cipher a mean mug before driving off.

Cipher laughed, amused by the show.

I hopped into Cipher's car quickly, and Cipher climbed behind the wheel.

"You all right, Mai?"

"I'm cool," I replied, brushing that weird feeling off me. "Let's roll, baby."

"What you feel like doing?"

"Let's drink, get high, and fuck."

"Damn. I got it like that?"

"Hell yeah. I'm always down for whatever."

He had the cutest grin on his face as he nodded and peeled off.

Chapter 5

Troi

Six weeks later . . .

"You look surprised. Was this not planned?" The doctor stared at me oddly through her glasses.

I'd been afraid that the flutters and the nausea were more than the flu, and I was right.

"I'm more than surprised. I'm mortified."

"Were you not using birth control?"

"I usually take the pill, but my ex-fiancé was in jail for nine months, so I stopped taking them. He came home six weeks ago, and we had sex, but we broke up. I've never, *ever* been pregnant before."

"Well, you're having a baby. Congratulations."

Congratulations wasn't the word I wanted to hear. I was actually in mourning, and as far as I was concerned, a minister's prayer before burying a dead body six feet under would have been more apropos. I mean, why in the world would I want to be another one of Rocko's baby mamas? This had to be some sick joke God was playing on me.

The rest of the doctor's appointment was a blur, and whatever the doctor said went in one ear and out the other. I was there in the flesh, but I wasn't there mentally.

On the drive home, I felt even sicker, because this wasn't a dream. I was pregnant. I called Rocko to tell him the news, but he didn't answer. After a minute, he called back.

"Hello?" I said.

"Hey, Troi. How are you?"

"I'm all right, I guess. What are you doing?"

"About to take my little girl to the zoo. What are you doing?"

I paused. He was spending time with his daughter. I realized that I wasn't paying attention to where I was driving. My thoughts had gotten me off track, and I had missed the freeway ramp toward home.

"I . . . um . . . nothing much. Can we talk face-to-face?"

"Is everything okay?" he asked.

"Yeah. Um, how close are you to the zoo? I can be there in about sixteen minutes."

"I'm about twenty minutes away."

"Okay. I'll be in the parking lot across from the zoo," I said.

"All right."

I hung up and made a U-turn to head toward the freeway. I got off on Sutterville and drove to the zoo. I found a parking spot underneath some shady trees, turned off the car, and rolled down all the windows so the soft breeze could hit me in the face. That air felt so refreshing, but it wouldn't stop the tightness from seizing my damned throat. I tried to fight the tears silently, but I lost my own battle. I really broke down and cried while I sat and watched mothers push strollers and hold their small children's hands. I wasn't ready to trade in my Coach purse for a diaper bag.

Right when Rocko pulled up next to me, I had nearly lost myself in my tears, but I quickly pulled myself together. He got out of the car and opened his back door.

After he closed the door, he came over to my side of the car with his little girl resting on his shoulder.

"Come on. Let's talk," he said.

I rolled up the windows and hopped out. "What's her name?" I asked in a low voice, as if I were afraid to ask.

"Niara Nicole Cooper."

She was one of the most gorgeous little girls I had ever laid eyes on. She made me instantly wonder if our child would be just as breathtaking. I shook the thought out of my head, because I wasn't sure if I even wanted to have a baby yet.

"She's adorable, Rocko. I see you're doing what you need to do."

"It was time. It's actually been time, but, anyway, let's talk."

"Okay."

He walked toward the crosswalk, and I walked with him.

"I had a doctor's appointment this morning," I revealed.

"You did? Why? Is everything okay?"

"No, everything is not okay. I'm pregnant, and it's all your fault."

He smirked and then chuckled. "That is not all my fault. You knew you hadn't taken your birth control pills, and you knew the day I would be home, so . . ."

I cringed. "This is some bull . . ." I stopped myself before I could curse, because of his daughter.

He paid the admission for us to get into the zoo. "I know you don't want to hear this, but I do love you, and I want us to be back together. I don't want to have another baby without being in a relationship."

"What about your obligations to your other kids? Won't this stretch you too much?"

"I'm flexible, baby. You know I'll make the necessary adjustments."

I hissed and sucked my teeth. My mind couldn't focus on being positive, because I was still pissed at him for cheating on me. "Well, I'm not keeping the baby, Rocko. That's what I want to tell you."

He frowned deeply. "I don't believe in abortions, so you getting rid of my baby is out of the question."

"Is that what you told the others? You know what? Don't answer that. I really don't care what you believe in at this point."

"You know, I keep thinking about what you said about being honest. You were right. My children are a part of me, and I had no right to keep them a secret from you. I still have a responsibility, so even if we don't work out, I'll still be there for our baby too. Please don't kill it."

I tried not to cry again, but it didn't work. Tears ran down my cheeks. "I don't deserve this. I'm a good woman."

After observing my tears, he looked deep into my eyes. "Troi, you're the best woman I've ever known, and I want to spend the rest of my life with you. I'm sorry, babes, for fucking things up."

I wanted to believe him, but I couldn't. "I want to have a baby with my husband."

"So marry me, then."

"You're a liar and a cheater," I reminded him.

"All I need is one more chance to prove to you that I can be faithful."

"Nope."

"Well, then, at least don't kill my baby. Think about it before you decide, please."

I tried to keep my eyes on the giraffes, but every time I looked at his daughter's face, the only thing I could think about was how much he had lied to me about her.

Chapter 6

Heather

Rocko dropped Niara off around nine o'clock on Sunday night. I was so excited to see that not only was she in one piece, but he also had her looking so cute in her new outfit and smelling like a princess should. After I put her in her pajamas, I tucked her into bed. Right before I could lie down, the phone rang. I looked down at the screen. Why was Rock calling when he had just left?

I answered, "Did you forget something?"

"Nah, I didn't forget anything. Do you have time to talk, or is Jared going to get mad again?"

I ran my left hand through my short, curly hair and blew air from my lips. He was starting to get on my nerves already. "What do you want now, pest?"

"Oh, I'm a pest now?"

"Yes, you're a pest, Rocko, and I'm not in the mood. Hurry up and tell me what you want."

"I took Niara to the zoo early this afternoon with Troi."

Tension consumed my lower neck as I sat down on my bed. Why did Rocko have that woman around my child? I massaged my neck with my left hand. "Okay . . ."

"I want to be the first one to tell you that she's pregnant."

I pulled my legs up to my torso, feeling weird about this conversation. "Okay."

"I don't know how to get her back, Heather. She loved me more than any other woman has."

He was wrong about that. I had loved him unconditionally at one time. What he should've said was that he loved her more than he had ever loved anyone else.

"She wants to have an abortion," he added.

"Well, damn, do you blame her?"

"I don't, but then again, my child deserves life. You know how I feel about abortions. I want to marry her, Heather."

I shrugged my shoulders. I used to wonder if he ever really wanted to get married, since they had been engaged without a wedding date for so long. When he'd started sleeping with Mai behind her back, I'd wondered if he knew how to be with one woman.

"So, what's stopping you from marrying her?"

"She done with me. What am I supposed to do?"

"If you really love her, you'll let her breathe. If she wants to forgive you, then you have to let her do that on her own time."

"What if that doesn't work?"

"Then you have to be okay with moving on."

"Can I ask you something?"

"Yeah."

"How come Jared hasn't asked you to marry him?"

I paused. Where did that question come from? I rubbed the top of my knees. I didn't want him in my personal business. If he wanted to tell me about what was going with him, that was fine.

"He's asked me, but I'm not going to discuss that with you," I replied.

"So, he has asked you?"

"Look, we're not talking about this."

"All right. Thank you again for allowing me to spend time with my baby. She's so precious."

"I'm glad you enjoyed her. It seems like she had fun."

"We had a blast. Kiss her good night for me."

"I will."

"Good night, Heather."

"Good night." I hung up the phone and tapped my fingernails on top of my knees.

I thought about the time Jared had proposed right after Niara was born. I had told him no because I hadn't been over the pain Rocko caused me. I thought he was afraid to ask me again because my first response had crushed him.

Jared was more than my lover and friend. He was like a savior to me. He took care of my heart by treating it as if it were a delicate flower. I owed my life to him, because he had come along when I'd given up on love. He had shown me what real love was supposed to feel like, and I didn't have any regrets about us.

Chapter 7

Mai

I was making the baby a bottle when Cipher called. A huge grin appeared on my face when I saw Cipher's name flashing on my phone. I loved the way he made me feel every time he looked at me. I liked hanging out with him because it came with some benefits, like a little shopping, dinner, and a little cash here and there.

"Hey, sexy," I said as sensually as I could manage.

"What you doing tonight?"

I sighed and rolled my eyes. "I can't do anything. I have school in the morning."

"Oh, yeah, that's right. I keep forgetting you've gone back to school. Will you be free this weekend?"

"Hell yeah. It's my birthday."

"I know. I've been planning a little something special. Are you down to being kidnapped?"

"I'm always down to being kidnapped by you. I can't wait to see you."

"Baby, you know I feel the same way about you. Do I get to have you for the whole weekend or what? I want to taste you."

"Once you get a taste, you'll be sprung for life. I'm warning you now."

He hummed into the phone. "Is that right? Check this out, Mai. I gotta tend to some business right now, but I promise to hit you up a little later. Is that cool?"

"Yeah."

"All right. I'll call you in a little bit."

I finished making the bottle and put the cap on it. Before I could see what was on TV, the doorbell rang. Neiosha was waiting at the screen door for me to let her in.

"I don't answer the door for tricks," I joked as I approached the door.

"Open the door, ho," she replied and laughed.

I unlocked the screen door and held it open, and she walked in wearing a red miniskirt and a tight-fitting yellow top that showed off some major cleavage from her double-D breasts. Neiosha's style was always wild and crazy, but she looked cute as she flung her long, straight weave over her shoulder.

"Girl, your hair is supercute," I said.

She looked around the house. "Thank you. What you doing?"

"About to feed the baby."

"Where's he at?"

"Down for a nap, but he should be waking up any minute."

"You really going back to school tomorrow?" she asked as she sat on the couch.

"Yup, and I already can't wait until I'm done."

"At least you're going back. That takes major determination. I commend you on doing what you have to do."

I smiled. "Aw, thank you."

"Sooo, best friend," she said, "what's this I hear about you creeping with my boo, Cipher? Tell me that shit ain't true?"

The deep frown on her face told me that she wasn't feeling it. I hadn't thought she would care, because she had too many niggas on her line to be worried about Cipher, and now she had me feeling nervous.

"Where you hear that?" I asked and cleared my throat.

She looked at me as if I had a problem. "Don't play dumb with me."

"I'm not playing dumb."

"So then, don't lie to me. We don't get down like this. Cipher is my piece, and you know that."

"Does he know that he's your piece?"

She stood to her feet. "I was with my piece last night."

I shifted my weight to my right leg. "Seriously?"

"I'm dead serious."

"He didn't tell me, and he knows you're my best friend."

"That nigga ain't gonna tell you. That's why I'm telling you now. Why would he tell you when he can have his cake and eat it too? You already know what's up, but you don't care about anybody else but yourself."

"Please, don't try to do me like some heartless ho. Cipher wouldn't play us against one another."

"Bitch, please. He's doing it, and you're letting him. The only reason I give him space from time to time is that he's still messed up over his cousin's death."

"He told me that his cousin died a few years ago, but he didn't seem too bothered by it."

"Do you know what happened to his cousin?"

"Some gang shit, right? I never really asked him. I just heard about it."

"Maybe you should ask him. Better yet, why don't you ask Rocko?"

I scowled. "Why would Rocko know anything about Cipher's cousin's murder?"

"Ask him. If he doesn't want to tell you, then ask Cipher."

I stared at her because I didn't understand why his cousin's murder was so important, but if Rocko had something to do with it, that would explain why Cipher had stared at him like he wanted to kill him.

Neiosha's eyes turned cold as she sat on the couch again. "I'm not playing with you, Mai. Cipher is off-limits. Don't make me have this conversation with you again."

"Look, girl, if you don't want me to fuck around with him anymore, I won't."

"Good, because we're supposed to be best friends, and best friends don't screw over friends for some dick."

Cipher would never choose her over me, and she knew that. That was why she was laying on the best friend thing so thick. She was acting like they were in love or something.

"Why did you tell me that you weren't really feeling him if you are?" I asked her.

"I wasn't feeling him at first, but that was before I got to know him better. I've been seeing him for two years now. Did you know that?"

"Two years? How come you never told me? Am I supposed to be a mind reader?"

"Did you ask me before you hopped on his dick?"

"No, but—"

"But nothing." She rolled her eyes. "You should've asked me off top."

"Well, he's supposed to be taking me out for my birthday this weekend, but I'll be sure to let him know I can't go."

"Good, because I don't care if he pulled his dick out in front of your mothafuckin' face and asked you to suck it. You will say no because you're my best friend."

"Okay. I got you."

She grunted and asked, "You whup on your baby daddy's bitch for beating your ass yet?"

Now she was trying to piss me off. "That bitch knows to stay on her side of the tracks."

"You should've never fucked with his ass in the first place when you knew he had a bitch."

Oh, now I was steaming. She had succeeded in pissing me the fuck off. "I have to get up early, so I should get to bed."

She stood up and pulled down her miniskirt. "Bye, bestie."

"Talk to you later," I replied.

As she walked out, Rocko was pulling up to the curb. He got out of the car and walked toward my screen door. He had a walk that always made his swagger extra sexy, but I tried my hardest not to notice.

I walked out of the house and stood on the front lawn to greet him.

"Where's my son?" he asked.

"He's in the house, sleeping. What do you want?"

"I came to check on him."

"Well, you got to come back tomorrow, because I'm not waking him up. Where you coming from?"

Rocko frowned, as if I had no business asking him about his whereabouts. He walked past me to the screen door and let himself in, as if I had invited him. I followed him inside.

He sat on the couch, clasped his hands together, and wore a disgusted look on his face. "So, you really fucking around with Cipher?"

I looked up at the ceiling. What in the hell was going on with all the questioning about Cipher? Between him and Neiosha, I didn't know who got on my nerves the worst.

"I don't know why you and everyone else cares so much about what I'm doing. Cipher doesn't have anything to do with you. What's the real problem? You jealous?"

"Fuck no. Thanks to your big-ass mouth, everyone knows we have a son together, and I don't trust just anyone around him."

"As long as our son has me, he'll always be good. You don't need to worry about him being around anyone janky."

"You don't get it."

"What is there to get?" I asked.

"I handle things a certain way to protect the people I care about. Since you find a way to violate that in every way you can, now I gotta be on guard. I won't even get into the calls you made to my phone to set Troi off."

"You decided to stick your dick inside of me, so that's your fault. I don't give a fuck about your so-called relationship. You don't know how to be good to nobody. Period."

"Shut the fuck up and listen. You're so busy trying to hop on Cipher's dick that you don't see the danger you're putting you and my child in. He's not who you think he is, so keep your eyes open."

"Well, who is he to you, Rocko? Since you know him so well."

"That's none of your business. All you gotta do is do what I tell you to do. End of story."

"I think you're jealous of him."

He said with a chuckle, "You're so young and dumb."

"Since you think I'm so young and dumb, your ass can leave." I pointed to the front door.

"I was trying to have an adult conversation with you, but that's impossible. I'm gone. Oh, before I leave, I'm going to start taking my son for two days a week. Wednesdays and Thursdays."

"Why? So you can have him around Troi?"

"Don't be childish. This is about me spending time with my son."

"No, you won't be taking him anywhere. If you want to spend time with him, you'll spend time with him right here."

"I swear, having a baby with you was the wrong fucking thing to do. You make me regret this shit more and more every day."

Tears flooded my eyes. "I never asked you to take off the condom."

"No, but you sure did lie about being on Depo, didn't you? If I'd known you weren't really on the shot, I would've never gone raw."

"Fuck you, Rocko!"

He stood up to leave. "I'm coming to pick up my son tomorrow."

"Don't come up over here."

He shook his head and walked out of the house.

My tears fell like hard rain, and my chest heaved up and down.

When I turned around, my mother was glaring at me. I stormed off to my room as my tears rushed down both of my cheeks. I didn't understand why Rocko couldn't give me the same respect he gave Heather and Troi.

Chapter 8

Troi

I sat in the lobby at the clinic, waiting to be called to terminate my pregnancy. I rocked a little, with my arms folded across my middle as the pit of my stomach was hurting. I was nervous, afraid of the procedure. Rocko was blowing my phone up because he didn't want me to go through with it, but I had to do what I had to do without him in my damn ear.

I stared at the pregnant women who were waiting on their checkups. They seemed happy with their decision to keep their babies. Pregnancy was supposed to be a beautiful thing. It was the miracle of life, the wonder of creating another human. I was supposed to be welcoming a new being into my heart and soul. One woman walked in, looking as if she were ready to pop. She looked as if her body had been stretched to the limits and she was in great discomfort. If I kept the baby, could I handle the hormonal changes and the body transformation? Could I nurture and carry a growing baby?

Another pregnant woman came in, holding a toddler by the hand, and checked in at the counter. I watched them as they sat down. The toddler was beyond cute, and he was smiling with bright eyes. He had the cutest dimples in each cheek. Guilt washed over me instantly. Why would they put everyone in the same room like this?

Was this a method to make the women who were considering not having their children change their minds? I was already feeling strange after driving up and seeing all the picketers out front protesting abortions. What was I doing?

"Troi Anderson."

I hopped up and followed the nurse. The nurse took me to a tranquil room with lit candles, soft music, a few tiny bonsai waterfalls, and a fish tank.

She spoke in a voice slightly above a whisper. "In this room, you'll relax while you wait on the doctor. I'm going to give you Valium and some water to help calm your nerves. So, have a seat, and I'll be right back."

I sat down on the couch, took a deep breath, and stared at the fish tank. I listened to the water flowing through the filter, along with the soft music. Already, I was beginning to relax, but then sadness overcame me, as I could see nothing but the little boy with the dimples smiling at his mother. I closed my eyes, and tears escaped from my burning eyelids. I wiped them away quickly.

The nurse returned and gave me the Valium. I took the pill with a tiny cup of water.

"Try your best to relax. The doctor will call you in about ten minutes," the nurse announced, then left the room.

I sank into the plush couch and closed my eyes. I thought about the women I had seen in the lobby, and my heart felt conflicted. I had never before been in a position to do anything like this. What if this was my only chance to have a baby? I had heard about women not being able to conceive again after they had an abortion. I touched my stomach and cried. I couldn't go through with this. I couldn't kill my baby and ruin my shot of being a mother. I hopped off the couch, made my way back to the lobby, and left the clinic.

Chapter 9

Heather

After Thursday morning's class, I got a call from Niara's day care to let me know that Jared hadn't picked her up. That meant she had been there thirty minutes longer than expected. I was pissed as I raced there to get her. Ever since Rocko had started coming every other weekend to get Niara, Jared had been acting weird. I wanted them to hash out their differences. I mean, I didn't expect them to go back to being as close as they once were, but I expected them to show some sort of respect for one another and to get along for Niara's sake.

After I picked up Niara, I tried calling Jared, but he didn't answer his phone. I hoped nothing bad had happened to him, so I went to his place after grabbing some food. Once I walked inside, I sat the food on the kitchen counter. I took off Niara's jacket and put my backpack on the couch.

"Jared? Are you home?" I called.

The apartment was quiet, so I looked out the window to see if his car was in his stall. It wasn't. I hadn't noticed while I was walking in that it was gone.

I sent him a text. Hey, babe. I picked up Niara, and we're at your house, chilling.

Next, I turned on the TV. One of those court shows was on. All the court cases were alike, and this one was yet another paternity case, but the episode was entertaining enough to keep my attention. During the first commercial break, I went into the kitchen and retrieved Niara's fries and my cheeseburger. While we were eating, I heard a faint sound, so I turned down the TV.

The sound of Beyoncé's song "Naughty Girl" was coming from Jared's bedroom. I walked into his bedroom. Jared's cell phone was lighting up and ringing on the nightstand. I had never heard that Beyoncé ringtone on his phone before. I looked around the room, and I saw that it wasn't how he usually left it before he went to work. The bed was a mess. In plain view on the tossed covers at the foot of the bed was an empty gold condom wrapper. My heart stopped. He hadn't managed to pick up my daughter, because he had been fucking someone else. Beyoncé was still singing from the nightstand. I picked up the cell phone and stared in disbelief at the name Angel on the screen. I had never heard of her. I hadn't had a reason to suspect Jared of cheating, and I hadn't felt insecure, so this discovery came as a shock.

I took his phone into the living room and sat down, trying my best to figure out why he would do this to me. Three text messages came through from Angel while his phone was in my hand, but I couldn't read them, because his phone was locked. My palm began to itch because I knew the code. I wanted to read those messages so badly, but I was afraid of what they said. I punked out as I marched to his bedroom, where I put the phone back on the nightstand. I wanted him to know that I had seen his room this way, so I opened the window to let in some fresh air. I picked up the empty gold condom wrapper and placed it on his dresser. Then I removed the bedclothes, put the sheets in the wash, and put fresh sheets on the bed.

As I was walking back into the living room, Jared came in through the garage with a bag of food from Maria's Tacos in his right hand.

"What you doing here, babe?" he asked when he saw me.

"I came to check on you since you didn't pick up Niara. I called you, but you didn't answer."

"Damn, yeah, my bad. I left my phone here. I would've gotten you something if I knew you were coming."

"We got some food."

He didn't speak to Niara, and she didn't seem too concerned about it, as she continued to eat her food. He walked to his bedroom and paused in the doorframe.

I walked up behind him, saying, "Your cell phone was ringing while you were gone."

He stepped into the room and picked up his cell from the nightstand. He didn't look at it. Instead, he stuck it straight in his jeans pocket before flopping on the bed.

"You notice anything different about your room?" I asked.

"No."

"You should. It was a mess before you left, so I cleaned it up for you. I changed the sheets and everything."

"Thanks."

I folded my arms across my chest and asked, "Who's Angel?"

"I don't know. Why?" He frowned, as if he'd never heard that name before.

"You know who Angel is. Your naughty girl."

He didn't respond. He opened his bag from Maria's Tacos, took out a taco, bit into it, and chewed. It was almost as if I wasn't talking to him.

"Jared, her number is saved in your phone, and you set a ringtone for her, Beyoncé's "Naughty Girl," to be exact."

"Babe, you're tripping. I don't know anyone named Angel, and I definitely don't have a Beyoncé ringtone on my phone."

Was he going to sit there and lie through his teeth?

I fluttered my eyelashes. "Really? Are you seriously going to lie to my face like that? I know what I saw and heard."

"How can I lie about something when I don't even know what you're talking about?"

I walked out of the bedroom, went into the bathroom, locked the door, and cried because I couldn't believe he would lie so easily. I should've called her back while I had the chance.

"Heather," I heard him say from outside the door. "Why are you crying?"

"Leave me alone, Jared. Out of all the places, you brought someone here, to the same bed we make love in."

"Open the door, Heather. I want to talk to you."

I didn't deserve any of this. Not again, and not from a man I had put all my hope and faith in. I opened the door.

He stared at my face but didn't say anything.

"Jared, I found a condom wrapper in there." I went into the bedroom and retrieved the wrapper from the top of his dresser and showed it to him.

"Oh, I see what's going on. My brother brought some chick over. He couldn't take her to my mom's house, so I let him use my room. They must've left before you got here."

I frowned, because he must've thought I was stupid. I tossed the wrapper back on the dresser.

His phone vibrated loudly in his pocket. Slick bastard turned off the ringer. He sat down on the bed and continued to eat his food, unbothered.

"Jared, who's calling you?"

"Doesn't matter. I don't want to talk to anyone, not when I'm having an important discussion with the woman I love."

"Give me your phone," I demanded, with my hand extended.

"Why?"

"Because I said so."

"No. You want to talk about something that's bothering you, so let's talk."

"Are you cheating on me?" I asked as my lips quivered.

"You got the wrong nigga."

"Is that a yes or a no?"

He continued to eat his food.

I frowned deeply. "So, Angel wasn't here?"

"No one was here today but me."

"I thought you said your brother was here with some chick. Which is it? You were here alone, or was your brother here?"

"Doesn't matter. You're going to believe whatever you want."

"The condom, the messy bed, the fucked-up odor, the singing phone, and your lies. All of that is enough to tell me that you're a liar. I'm not doing this."

I stormed out of the bedroom, then grabbed Niara's hand, my backpack, and her coat.

"Mommy, where we going?"

"We're going home, baby. Is that okay with you?" I said as we left the apartment.

"Yeah. Can I have some candy?"

"We have some fruit cups at home."

Just then a young, light-skinned woman with long, bouncy curls walked out of the apartment below Jared's. I had seen her a few times before, but we had never spoken. She headed toward the parking lot.

A man yelled from the apartment, "Angel, you left your phone."

As she walked toward the man behind the cracked open door, her belly button ring reflected the sun's rays, and her hazel eyes scanned mine for a split second. A small smile appeared on her pouty, glossed lips as she threw on her Dolce & Gabbana sunglasses. She flipped her wavy hair before going inside.

Her name was Angel? Was Jared fucking his neighbor?

Chapter 10

Rocko

My phone rang as I was driving to my crib. Finally, Troi was calling me back. I had been worried sick about her, and I had been hoping to catch her before she ended our baby's life.

I picked up on the second ring. "Troi," I said, "please tell me you didn't do it."

"Sorry I didn't call you back sooner."

"Okay. What's good?"

"I didn't do it, because I couldn't do it."

I heaved a sigh of relief. "You all right?"

"I'm fine. I got to thinking about it, and all those women were in there with their little cuties, and I just couldn't bring myself to kill our baby."

"That makes me feel so much better. You sure you're all right?"

"Yeah, I'm sure. I just called to tell you that."

"I appreciate it."

"Okay. Talk to you later."

"Later." I wanted to say more, to tell her how much I loved her, but she was sick of hearing it since my actions hadn't matched my words.

Though she had kept our conversation brief, the dark cloud I felt had lifted. She was going to give me a shot at being her baby daddy.

As I pulled into my garage, my dad pulled up behind me. I shut off the car and got out.

He climbed out and walked into my garage. "Hey, son."

"What's good, Pop?" I asked.

He looked worried as he said, "You got time to holler at ya old man?"

"Yeah. Come inside."

We walked into the house, and I pressed the button to close the garage door.

"What's this I hear about Mai and Cipher?" he asked, not wasting any time.

The streets talked, and although Pop was no longer thugging, the OG in him kept his ear to the streets, especially since his son was the prince of his old stomping grounds.

"I keep telling her to leave that nigga alone, but she's hardheaded."

"Does she know about your history with him?"

"Kind of, but not really." I rubbed the top of my head.

"So, why don't you stop pussyfooting around the issue?"

"Because there are things she shouldn't know," I said with a shrug. "My past dealings with Cipher are none of her fucking business. She should just listen to what the fuck I tell her to do."

Pop shook his head. "I think if she knew, she wouldn't fuck with him. That girl is crazy about you."

"Pop, if she's so crazy about me, why does she do the shit she do? She walks around like she's clueless. The bitch ain't street smart and will get a nigga killed. She does things purposely to fuck with me because I didn't choose her over Troi. She uses him to try to make me jealous, but I ain't never that."

"You think he's still tripping off Greg?"

"He shouldn't be, but I can see it in his eyes. The nigga moves weird around me."

"Watch your back. I don't trust him, and you gotta make sure Mai isn't saying or doing anything that will get you fucked up. I'll ride for mine, so don't make the retired nigga come back out. You hear me?"

I nodded. "I hear you, Pop. Don't worry. I'll take care of it."

"Get that girl and your baby out of Oak Park quick."

I thought about it. He was right. I needed to take her out the hood. My son deserved a chance. "I got the perfect spot in Elk Grove. I'll go see about it tomorrow morning."

"Good. Whatever you do, stay strapped and lay low. It's hot, and people are talking mad shit about Greg's murder case being opened back up. You hear about that?"

"Nah, I didn't."

Pop pointed at his ear and gave me a look that said that I better wake the fuck up. "I'm going home. Holler if you need me."

"I will."

We hugged before I walked him out the front door. Pop had brought this to me because it was important for me to do what I needed to do to protect myself and my family. I went to the safe and took some money out. I had the perfect plan to get Mai and my son out of the hood for good.

Chapter 11

Mai

Cipher was the only person I wanted to spend my birthday with. I didn't care what Rocko or Neiosha was talking about. I was living my best life. Cipher kept me up late at night and gave me all the passion that I craved. I was working hard to graduate and earn my degree, and I needed someone to help me relax. Cipher attended to me and my needs in a way Rocko never could. I wasn't going to say that I was in love with Cipher, but I was getting closer to the feeling.

"Bye," I said, hopping out of Cipher's car.

"Thank you for chilling with me. I had so much fun with you."

"I had fun too."

"Make sure you call me," he said.

"I'll call you later."

"All right."

I went into the house. My mom was gone with the baby, so I had time for myself for once. As soon as I flopped down on the couch and turned on the TV, my phone started ringing. It was Neiosha. I rolled my eyes and sighed as I answered, "Hey, girl."

"Don't 'Hey, girl' me. Why I just see Cipher leaving your house?"

"Cipher? Leaving here? I don't think so," I lied quickly.

"Come outside." She hung up in my face and honked her horn, letting me know she was right outside my house.

My heartbeat quickened. Neiosha was notorious for beating on girls. She always fought dirty. She carried a razor blade under her tongue and would pull out a padlock from her bra. If she didn't fight alone, she brought her two big cousins to stomp a bitch into the concrete. I looked out the blinds to see whether she was alone. I wasn't about to go outside, though. There was no way I would fight her over a man who did whatever he wanted to do.

Neiosha called again. My mom was pulling into the driveway at that very moment, so I went ahead and answered because I felt safe. "I'm not coming outside."

"You can't bring your ass outside to talk to me?"

"Not right now."

"I better not catch your ass in the streets, scary-ass bitch." She pulled away quickly from the curb, making her tires screech.

Neiosha was nuts, but I knew that. She wasn't about to catch me anywhere. I opened the door for my mom, so she could bring some grocery bags in.

"Was that Neiosha driving crazy like that?" she asked.

I refused to answer her question. I asked, "Where's the baby?"

"He's asleep in the back seat. Get him, please."

I cautiously looked out the window, and when I saw the coast was clear, I walked out of the house barefoot to get my son. Once I had his seat unlatched, I lifted it out, shut the car door, and jogged back into the house. It didn't make sense to feel this paranoid.

As soon as I was inside the house again, I locked the door. I went over to the blinds and looked out once more. Just then Neiosha's car passed the house and she blew up my phone.

"Mai?" Mom said, with a concerned look on her face.
"Yeah?"
"What are you doing in my blinds like that?"
"Nothing," I replied, stepping away.
"When did you get home?"
"I just got here."
"What's going on?"
"Nothing." I picked up the baby out of his car seat, went to my bedroom, closed the door, and dialed Neiosha's number. The only thing I could think of was to call her and try to talk some sense into her. As the phone rang, I placed li'l Rocko in his crib.

She answered the call. "Mai, you're hella scandalous. I can't stand you."

"I'm not trying to be, Neiosh, but I'm feeling him."

"Ugh. Why can't you date somebody that doesn't belong to anybody? This is why you're always getting your ass beat. I'm fa sho' beating ya ass."

"I'm not going to fight you."

"Yes, you *are* going to fight me. You told me you wouldn't fuck with him anymore."

"But, Neiosh, Cipher won't stop texting me. What am I supposed to do? Especially since he said y'all ain't all that serious."

"Bitch, *what*? I'm not playing with you. Bring your ass outside."

"Look, I'll leave him alone if that will make you stop this nonsense."

"That's what you said the last time I was at your house."

"I promise this time I will."

She hung up the phone in my face.

I figured if anybody could make this stop, Cipher could, so I decided to call him.

"What's up, Mai?" he said when he answered.

"Neiosha is tripping. She—"

"Don't trip off her."

"Are you still fucking her?"

"Yeah. Is that a problem?"

I frowned. I had expected him to lie about it. His answer threw me off because he was so honest. "Why didn't you tell me?"

"'Cause you don't give a fuck about her."

I folded my arms across my chest, keeping the phone close to my ear. "I do care. She's my best friend."

He laughed hysterically. "You don't care a rat's ass about that bitch."

"That's not completely true. Look, we gotta stop seeing one another. She's mad at me."

"When has another broad stopped you from getting what you wanted?"

"What you trying to say?"

"I'm saying you rocked with Rocko, even though he had a bitch. You knew I was fucking with her, so now because she knows, we're not cool anymore?"

"That's exactly what that means."

"Stop it."

"I'm serious. My friendship with her means more to me at this point."

"I know how to take care of that pretty pussy, don't I? Relax. I got you, baby. She won't fuck with you anymore. Bet."

I melted because I didn't want to leave him alone, and I knew he could fix this problem. He was all mine every time we were together. "I don't need Neiosha giving me any problems."

"I got you. It's good. Come back out and kick it with me later tonight."

"Okay."

"All right. I'm about to smoke, so I'll call you right back."

"Okay."

I ended the call, walked out of my bedroom, went into the kitchen. My mother was standing at the stove.

"Mama?"

"Yeah?"

"What you making?"

"Some fish tacos. You want one?"

"Nah. You frying the fish?" I asked as I sat at the kitchen table.

"Yeah, for these tacos. You want a piece of fish or something?"

"Yeah, I'll take a piece."

"Okay. Are you going to take the test for your driver's license on Saturday?"

"Yeah. You work tonight?"

"I'm off. Why?"

"I'll be stepping out. Can you watch the baby?"

She gave me a stern look. "Don't go off messing around with Rocko. I'm not sitting at the hospital all night for you to get stitches again."

I sucked my teeth. She always had to bring that up every time I wanted to go somewhere. "I'm not going anywhere near Rocko."

The doorbell rang, and I jumped. I prayed it wasn't Neiosha. I made a dash to the front door, and when I looked in the peephole, I sucked my teeth. I had a bad habit of talking Rocko up.

"Oh, well, look who it is," I said as soon as I opened the door. "You coming back to argue with me some more?"

"No. Come outside for a minute."

I sighed and stepped out of the house. "What's up?"

He handed me a duffel bag. "Here. I need you to put this up in a safe place for me. You think you can do that?"

"What's in here?"

"Money, so don't spend it. I'm not giving it to you. I'm asking you to hold on to it for me."

I raised my eyebrows. "This is money?"

He looked into my eyes. "Can you be a big girl and hold this for me? I would put it in the safe in my house, but I really don't want to keep this stash there."

"What you do? Rob a bank?"

He looked around, as if someone would hear him. He said quietly, "Put that in a safe place for me. Do not spend a dime of it. You hear me? Did you get your driver's license yet?"

"Not yet. I have an appointment at the DMV on Saturday."

"Good. I got you a car."

"What? For real? What kind?"

"A Lexus. If you pass the test on Saturday, I'll deliver it to you."

I didn't like the way he sounded when he said that. Something was wrong.

"What's going on, Rocko?"

He rubbed his goatee and stared intensely into my eyes. "I need you to handle this, okay?"

"Does this have anything to do with the police opening up Cipher's cousin's case?"

Frowning, he replied immediately, "Stop listening to what people are saying out here in the streets, especially if it's coming from Cipher. Don't believe anything he tells you. You hear me?"

"I wouldn't have to listen if you just tell me yourself."

"Stay focused." He handed me a key. "This is for a brand-new condo I got for you and my son. Don't worry about the rent or bills. I got you. I'll text you the address."

"Rocko, you're scaring me. Why you talking like you're about to go away for a long time? You going back to jail or something?"

"Stop with all the questions, Mai." His brows went down, causing deep lines to form in his forehead. He looked like I was stressing him out.

"All right. You heading to the bay tonight?" I said.

"Yeah, I gotta pick up Niara."

"Okay." I paused, thinking about my love life. I wanted a man all to myself, and I didn't like to share. "Can I ask you something?"

"Sure."

"Am I girlfriend material?"

"Are you asking generally or for a specific person?"

"I feel like men see me only as someone just to kick it with. No one has ever asked me to be their girlfriend before."

He rubbed his chin as he replied, "I think you'd be a cool girlfriend if you lose the fucked-up attitude."

"So, if you weren't with Troi, would you have asked me to be your girlfriend?"

"You and I don't mix. We're incompatible. We could never be together, but that doesn't mean that you won't find the right person to blend with."

"Okay."

"I want you and my son out of Oak Park ASAP. No one can know where your new condo is. Cipher, most definitely, isn't allowed to know. You got that?"

"Yeah, I got it. I can have the condo all to myself?"

"It's all yours. Do you mind if I see my son before I head out?"

"No, I don't mind. Come on."

He followed me into the house. I hurried to my bedroom and put the duffel bag deep in my closet. Li'l Rocko was stirring in his crib, so I picked him up. When we came out of the bedroom, my mom was staring at Rocko with her usual mean glare as they stood facing each other in the living room.

"Hello, Ms. Leslie," Rocko said.

She rolled her eyes. "Don't come up in here acting crazy today. I'm not in the mood for your shit."

He shook his head. "I promise I'm not here to cause any trouble."

I handed him the baby, and he sat on the couch.

Mama walked back into the kitchen, and I sat on the love seat adjacent to the couch. While Rocko talked to the baby and bounced him on his lap, I smiled on the inside. I had never thought Rocko would come around when he got out of jail. I was glad he wanted to be a part of his son's life, but I was in my feelings, because deep down, I wanted to be with Rocko.

Chapter 12

Troi

With my State of California badge, I clocked out of work at the time clock, feeling dead tired. I was okay with my decision to keep my baby, but being pregnant had me feeling off-balance. I had fallen asleep at my desk a few times today. As soon as I was out of the building, I checked my cell. Rocko had texted me a few times, telling me how happy he was that I was going to have our baby. I rolled my eyes. Yes, I was having his baby, but that didn't mean we were getting back together.

Before I could get into my car, Erika pulled up alongside me, her car window down.

"Hey," she said, smiling.

"What's up, cow?"

She laughed and replied, "You're the cow now. I still can't believe you're going to be a mommy."

I took a deep breath and exhaled. "I know, right? What are your plans this weekend?"

"Rest and relaxation. What you doing?"

"Shopping for maternity clothes. I'm getting red marks on my stomach from all my pants being too tight."

She laughed and shook her head. "Your belly is growing fast all of sudden. You talk to Rocko yet about it?"

"Yeah. He checks on me all the time." I opened the car door and placed my briefcase inside.

"Girl, you're about to have his baby. You already know how much he loves you."

"Does he really? He cheated on me."

"He's stupid, but that doesn't mean he doesn't love you. You're the only one he's ever proposed to."

"True, but I think that makes me the stupidest."

"No, it doesn't. At least he knows what he did wrong. Have your space, but I think you should get back together."

"Hell no. I'm tired of Rocko's shit. We have our ups and downs, but enough is enough. He knows how to reel me in, but I want him to value me enough to be honest about who he is and what he's doing."

"I hear you. Hey, you know Joe, the fine Italian in your department?"

I nodded. "What about him?"

"He asked me out for dinner tonight, so I might take him up on that offer."

"Girl, he's fine, fine. You should go. Have a good weekend. I'll call you later."

"Okay." She rolled up her window and drove away.

I got in the car and turned the radio up so Ne-Yo could flood my vehicle. He was so sick of love songs, and so was I, but I loved this song. I hopped onto Highway 99, heading south from Broadway. The traffic wasn't too bad. All I could think about was having this baby as a single mother. There was stop-and-go traffic on the highway, so I decided to call my mother to alleviate the frustration the congestion caused me. I turned down the radio and dialed her number. When she answered, I talked through the car's speakers.

"Mama, how are you?"

"Good. How are you feeling? Morning sickness yet?"

"Not really. I'm so sleepy. I fight all day to keep my eyes open."

In her Southern drawl, she replied, "I remember those days. Whew. Better you than me. So, the doctors say I have to have my eyes worked on again."

She was a diabetic, so she was continually getting some sort of surgery or new medication. That was a part of her disease.

"I'm sure everything is going to turn out fine."

"I don't want your nappy-headed brothers to tear up my house while I'm in the hospital. They don't take care of me the way they should."

"Want me to talk to them?"

"Yeah. I can't do it anymore. I'm too old for this. Tyson and his pregnant girlfriend are getting on my last nerve."

"You told me that the last time we talked. When she going home?"

"Tyson doesn't want her to go home. She's been here fighting with him every single day. I think she moved in behind my back. I'm tired of the shouting. The baby isn't even here yet, and she acting crazy as hell. This is why young kids shouldn't have babies. They are still not done with high school. Both just dumb as hell. He says if he doesn't get that scholarship, then he's going into the navy. Either way, he's giving her the sign that he'll be leaving her to raise that baby without him."

"Tyson has always wanted to go into the navy, because Daddy was in the navy."

"I know it. I don't want my baby to go, not while this world is in such a wreck."

"I don't think you should worry about him, Mama. He's going to make his own decisions."

"Yeah, and be like y'all daddy, leaving me to raise this baby for them, but I'm not raising another kid." She breathed heavily into the phone. Talking about Tyson had made her short of breath.

"Calm down, Mama."

"Troi, I wish Tyson and Tyus were as self-sufficient as you are. You're having a baby, and I don't have to worry about you."

Daddy had been dead for five years, and she was still upset about his sudden passing. She acted like he had purposely left her alone, when, in fact, he had had a heart attack.

"I do miss Daddy."

"Hold on . . ." She pulled the phone away from her ear and yelled, "No, I don't have any money, Tyus! You need to get your spoiled ass a job." She pressed the phone to her ear again and said, "Troi, I don't know how he got so spoiled."

"You don't? You carried him around until he told you he didn't want you to."

She grunted and sucked her teeth.

Traffic was now a mess. I was ten minutes away from home. These dumb drivers always waited until the last minute to jump out of the exit-only lane.

"I love you. Talk to you later," I said.

"I'll call you later. I love you too."

I ended the call. Traffic started moving a little better the closer I got to my exit. I wondered which gender my baby was going to be. I also started thinking about what I and my mother had talked about. I didn't want to raise my baby to be like my brothers. My mom had done the best she could without my father, but they'd needed him. My child was going to need Rocko, so I wasn't going to keep him or her away from him.

Chapter 13

Heather

Rocko came to pick up Niara for the weekend. I wasn't in the mood to talk to him, because I had been in my feelings over Jared, but he wanted to chat. I stared at him and thought about how handsome he looked with his perfectly lined goatee. He had always been good looking to me. I used to feel like I was so lucky to be with him, but when he'd cheated, I'd felt so low. Now I was feeling that same way with Jared.

Rocko's eyes met mine as he struggled to tell me what was on his mind. He was in some sort of trouble, but it wasn't like him to be afraid of anything or anybody, so I was curious to see what was eating at him.

"You okay?" Rocko asked, beating me to the punch.

"Yeah. What you want to talk about?" I wasn't about to talk to Rocko about my issues with Jared.

He cuddled with our daughter on the couch as she fell asleep. He was so gentle with her. I was staring at a softer Rocko, a side of him I thought I'd never see.

Before he could respond, my phone rang. I shook my head as soon as I saw that it was Mai calling.

"It's your other baby mama," I said.

"Don't tell her I'm over here."

I answered, "Hello?"

"Heather?" Mai asked.

"Hey, Mai," I replied. "What's up?"

"Is Rocko there by chance?"

"No. Why?"

"When he left here, he said he was going by there to pick up Niara, but he's not answering my calls, and I have something to ask him."

I motioned toward the phone, and he shook his head.

"He hasn't made it yet. You want me to tell him you called when he gets here?"

"No, I'll keep trying his cell."

She hung up before I could say anything else.

"Why aren't you answering that girl's calls?" I asked.

"I just saw her. Whatever it is can't be that serious. You sure you're okay? You don't look okay." I was sitting at the other end of the couch, close enough for him to examine my every expression. Just like I knew everything about him, he knew everything about me.

"Why you keep asking me that? I thought you said you had something to tell me."

"I do, but it can wait. Is everything cool with Jared?"

"Everything is . . . cool," I replied.

"Don't lie to me. I can see the pain all over your face."

"I guess I can't hide it. Jared and I broke up. He's fucking around with his neighbor."

"How you know?"

"I caught him."

I fought the tears that burned from deep within. I didn't want to cry in front of Rocko, but no matter how much I didn't want to, I did, anyway. I sobbed lightly at first, but as soon as his hand touched my shoulder, that was when the tears poured from me.

With Niara still in his lap, he inched over to me and then hugged me. "I'm sorry. Men are idiots. He probably just got caught up."

"Is that what happened to you when we were together? You got caught up?" It was as if what I had always wondered spilled out unconsciously.

Now that the question was out there, it was too late to take it back.

"Yeah, I got caught up. I fell in love with Troi at first sight. I didn't know what to do about it, because I was with you and we were having a baby. I didn't want to hurt you, but I wasn't man enough to tell you what was going on. I should've never let everything that happened happen. You're beautiful, and you loved me. I just got wrapped up."

I wiped the tears away quickly. My heart hadn't been the same since Rocko screwed me over. It wasn't fair to Jared to make him wait for me to love him the way he wanted me to.

"Thanks for telling me that," I said.

"No problem. Troi doesn't want to be with me. I feel like it's my karma, you know."

"Yeah. What you want to talk about?"

"I don't want to hide anything from you. I gotta lay low for a little while. You know how it is."

"Lay low? Why don't you get out of the game completely?"

"I plan on it soon. Trust me. I don't want you to worry, though. I have precious cargo, so I'm going to be safe." He paused. "Me and Niara going to head out now," he said as he held the little girl tighter and stood up.

"Wait," I heard myself say. "Stay for a while. I don't want to be alone right now, if you don't mind."

He looked confused, but then he looked as if he understood. He laid Niara on the love seat before sitting next to me on the couch. I placed my head on his shoulder. He ran his fingers through my short hair, and hot tears ran down my face. I brushed them away as quickly as they came. No matter how much I wanted the pain to leave, I couldn't stop my tears.

"Stop crying, Heather. I hate seeing you cry."

"I'm trying not to, but last week I was at Jared's place and found an empty condom wrapper on his bedroom floor. The bed was unmade, and the room smelled like sex mixed with a woman's perfume. He denied everything and said he had let his brother use his apartment."

He shook his head. "I'm sorry to hear that."

"I've never caught him in a lie that big before."

"I'm not surprised. Jared was the biggest player around our hood. He's never been a loyal kind of nigga."

"But he was different with me, but I guess I wasn't enough," I said.

"Don't think like that. We fucked up, but that doesn't mean you're not good enough. Why do you think I was so mad when you two hooked up?"

"I thought it was because he was your best friend."

"That had little to do with it. Jared threw me under the bus to swoop in on you, only to do the same thing. That's why I was pissed. He's been doing it this whole time. Trust me when I say that. He just finally got caught."

The thought that Jared could've been cheating on me the entire time made me sadder. I hadn't thought about that.

His gentle rub on my back became a deep massage. I closed my eyes. His hands felt good as he caressed me.

"Do you miss Troi?" I asked.

"Like crazy, but she doesn't want to get back together."

"But you still love her, right?"

"Yeah, but I'm willing to let her be. That's how much I love her."

I opened my eyes as I said, "You're in love with Troi, and I'm still in love with Jared."

He stopped massaging me before things went another direction. "I know . . . Hey, I'm going to get going, okay? You're going to be fine. You just need time."

I nodded, with tears nestled in my eyes. "Yeah." I walked Rocko and Niara to the door. "Good night. Thanks for the talk."

"Anytime. Night."

As soon as Rocko left with Niara, I felt like I needed closure with Jared. I wanted this to be over indefinitely.

I texted Jared. I'm coming by to bring back your key and to get mine.

Jared replied right away. I'm here. Come on.

I grabbed my keys, purse, and shoes and left my apartment. A few minutes later, I was on the road. When I pulled up into the parking stall at Jared's apartment complex, I saw Angel coming out of her apartment. I got out of my car and just stood there holding my breath as Angel's heels clicked against the pavement while she walked briskly to her car. I wanted to question her, but it was over between Jared and me, so there was no need.

She climbed into her car, backed out of her parking stall, and drove off. I watched her car until it had disappeared beyond the sliding gate. I took a deep breath and exhaled.

As I was about to walk away from my car, a good-looking, tall, dark-skinned man came out of Angel's apartment. He adjusted his baseball cap on his head before he locked the door. Then he walked toward the black Hummer parked next to my car. He had smooth-looking chocolate skin, a thin, neat mustache, and he was tall enough to be a basketball player. He wore blue jeans, a green T-shirt with Bob Marley on the front, and black tennis shoes.

Noticing my stare, he flashed me a quick pearly smile before saying, "Good afternoon."

"Good afternoon. You live here?"

He nodded. "Yeah, my girlfriend and I have been here for almost two years now. You live upstairs, right?"

"No. My boyfriend lives upstairs." I let that ease out of my mouth when Jared and I weren't together. It was going to take a while to stop saying it. "I mean, my ex-boyfriend. Your girlfriend's name is Angel, right?"

"Yeah. You met Angel?" he asked, raising his eyebrow.

"Not formally."

He turned and walked closer to me, and I couldn't help but see how nice looking he was up close.

What the hell did Angel want with Jared if she had a fine-ass man like him?

"My name is Dante."

"Hi, Dante. I'm Heather."

I shook his hand after he extended it toward me. He towered over me. He had to be at least six foot five.

"It's nice to meet you," he said.

"It's nice to meet you as well."

He went over to his Hummer, opened the door, took a packet of papers out of it, and locked it. Then he returned to his apartment. I couldn't help but wonder why Angel was cheating on him.

I walked up the stairs to Jared's apartment and knocked on the door.

Jared opened the door and said, "Hey."

"Hey." I handed him the key.

He took it from me and said, "Come in."

I walked in, and he closed the door behind me.

"I just want to say that I'm sorry," he said. "I shouldn't have lied to you. My brother wasn't here with his girl."

I nodded as tears came to my eyes. "You fucking with Angel from downstairs?"

"I was . . . but she's in a situation, and I'm over it."

"So I'm supposed to be okay with that?"

"No. I'm not telling you this to wash it away. I want to know if one day you can forgive me. I'm not ready to walk away from you and Niara."

"I need some time to think about it." I said, wiping my tears.

He nodded. "I understand." He handed me his key to my apartment.

I turned away from him and walked out the door. As much as I loved Jared, I wasn't one to be played with. I was done.

Chapter 14

Troi

"Dinner was good," Rocko said as we walked out of the Italian restaurant.

I had agreed to go to dinner with him after he'd begged and pleaded. I'd said yes to get him to leave me the hell alone. His persistence was annoying, but at the same time, I'd missed him. Ever since I'd decided to keep the baby, my hormones had had me feeling soft.

"It was good," I said.

The night air was cold for a summer night, but that was how it was sometimes in Sacramento. One minute hot, next minute cold. I was ready to get in the car. I zipped up the jacket I was wearing as my shoulders nearly touched my ears.

"Are you cold?" he asked, his eyes sparkling. His eyes had been shining all damned night.

"Hella," I replied as my teeth chattered.

We rushed to his truck. Once inside, he turned the heater on full blast, which caused chilly air to blow in my face. I turned the vents down so the air wouldn't make me colder. He pressed the button to warm the leather seats.

"It will be warm in a minute. Thank you for having dinner with me, Troi. It means a lot to me."

"No problem." I yawned. I wasn't much of a night owl, and being pregnant didn't help. "Are you enjoying your weekends with your daughter?"

"I love every minute of the time we spend together. Heather and I have a great understanding. Mama is watching her for me right now, but I'm picking her back up after I drop you off. Tomorrow I'm picking up Junior so we can all do something together with Pop."

I nodded and cringed at the same time. I wanted him to spend time with his kids, but I wasn't used to him talking so freely about them. His reality had been a tough pill to swallow.

He headed south on 99, and I felt my eyelids droop a little. It was so warm and cozy in his car that I fell asleep. I couldn't help it. Good food was in my stomach, and I felt content. I woke up as he was pulling into my driveway.

"Looks like I dozed off," I said.

"You did."

"Good night, Rocko," I said as I placed my hand on the door handle.

"Hold on. Let me open the door for you." He got out of the truck, ran around to my side, and opened the door for me.

"Thank you," I said as I stepped out.

He hugged me, and his cologne was heavenly, as always. He buried his head in my neck and placed his hand on my tummy. He rubbed it, as if he could feel our child inside of me. He lifted his head, and the dimple in his left cheek deepened as he bit on his lower lip.

"Things are really awkward between us, but I'm changing for the better, Troi. I've made some bad mistakes, and I'm man enough to own up to it. Trust me when I say I'll wait forever for you if I have to."

"You don't mean that."

"I mean every word. No matter what happens to me, know that I'll always love you."

I swallowed the hard lump that had formed in my throat. I was terrified to raise my baby alone. Being a single mother was demanding work—I had learned that from my mother—but I was also afraid that Rocko hadn't had enough time to change and wasn't up to the challenge of a loyal relationship. He was spending time with his kids, and that was great, but could he be faithful?

"If you love me so much, why you lie to me so many times? Why you fuck around with other women?" I quizzed.

"I was weak, and I don't have a good excuse. I couldn't come out and say I was running around, being stupid. I had a real problem."

"I don't think you'll ever change, Rocko. I think this is who you are. Why not be single, so you can see who you want without hurting anyone?"

"Because I am madly in love with you. You're the only woman I see spending the rest of my life with. I've learned from my mistakes, so I appreciate you for going hard on me and teaching me that lesson. You'll just have to see. I'll show you."

I nodded and replied, "Only time will tell. Good night, Rocko."

"Good night, Troi. I love you."

I went inside and closed the door behind me. As I rested my back against the door, I closed my eyes. Being around Rocko had stirred up old feelings. Being without him was lonely, but I needed to get out of those feelings. Rocko wasn't the only man in the world. He was going to have to do more than just say what he was doing. I needed to see that he had changed and that he was sticking to his promises.

Chapter 15

Mai

I waited at the women's clinic to get my Depo shot early in the morning. I was growing impatient because they were behind schedule that day. I hated waiting. How come doctors never ran on time? Shit, if I was late, they would make me reschedule.

Troi entered the office, walked up to the counter, and said, "My name is Troi Anderson. I have an appointment at two."

I held my breath because I wasn't expecting to run into her, especially not at the women's clinic. I sat back and hoped that she didn't see me, but it was wishful thinking. Our eyes met, but she quickly looked away. She sat on the other side of the room and looked around for a magazine to read. After crossing her legs, she bounced one over the other.

Her skin was radiant, and her hair was pressed perfectly and bouncy, but she was still fat. I rolled my eyes. What did Rocko see in her? She was stuck up. Her attitude stayed snobby, like she was so much better than everyone else. He must've liked bourgeois women.

"Troi Anderson," called the receptionist from behind the window.

She got up and went to the window. I strained to hear what was being said.

"Is this your first prenatal appointment?" the woman asked.

"Yes," Troi whispered, but I could still hear her.

"Fill these out and bring them back when you're done."

Were my ears deceiving me? She was pregnant?

"Mai Wesley," a nurse finally called.

I got up and followed the nurse briskly as my mind started racing. Was Rocko avoiding me because his precious jewel was pregnant?

Chapter 16

Heather

Jared called me. "Heather, can you come by? I need to talk to you," he said when I picked up.

I had spent most of my day relaxing. I'd given myself a facial and read a few chapters of a new book. I had tried my best to keep my mind off Jared and to do some self-care, so when he called, I felt like he was ruining my day.

"About what?" I asked, rolling my eyes.

"It's really important. Can you please come over?"

"I guess so."

"All right. See you when you get here."

I ended the call and took my time. I wasn't about to rush. And what was so important? After I made a sandwich and ate it, I drove over to his place.

When I pulled up to his complex, he was outside, sitting on the steps. I got out of the car and approached him.

"Thanks for coming," he said.

"You want to talk out here or inside?"

"We can go inside. Is Rocko dropping off Niara tonight?"

"Yeah."

"What time?"

"He usually comes around seven. Why?"

"Just asking," he said as he stared at a small moving van that had pulled up behind me and parked.

Dante hopped out of the van and lifted the back. Angel came out of her apartment, carrying a small box.

Jared froze as soon as he saw her. The look in his eyes when they made eye contact made me uneasy. She headed to the van, ignoring his stare. Jared kept watching her, as if he was waiting for her to say something to him.

I frowned deeply, trying to read his thoughts. Their chemistry was that of old lovers trying to figure out unresolved things. If she was what he wanted, why in the hell did he want to talk to me?

Jared headed up the stairs, and I followed him.

Once we were inside his apartment and the door was closed, I said, "Jared."

He looked distraught as he went over to the window to watch Angel.

I folded my arms across my chest and said again, "Jared."

He turned from the window and looked at me. His silent stupor didn't sit well with me.

"What's going on?" I asked, fluttering my eyelashes. "Why did you call me to come over here to talk?"

"Angel is moving out. I want her to be happy."

"So, you called me over here to tell me that she's moving out?"

"Angel and I have been friends for a long time, and—"

"How long have you been friends?"

He grimaced. "What?"

"You've been cheating on me this whole time, haven't you?"

I thought I saw tiny tears appear in his eyes, but they disappeared so quickly as he replied, "Heather, I don't want to lose you. Please, can we work this out?"

"When was the first time you slept with her?"

"Why does it matter?"

"What do you mean, why does it matter?"

"I'm not sleeping with her anymore. That's all that should matter, right?"

"How many times has she been in your bed?"

"That doesn't matter, either."

"When was the first time, Jared?"

He blew air from his lips and folded his arms across his chest. Now he was getting upset because I wouldn't let this go. I had learned a lot from being with Rocko, which was to follow my gut always, regardless of the outcome.

"About three years ago."

I shook my head and bounced my keys against my knee. "You know what? I thought about it, and I can't do this anymore. We're done, Jared." I turned and walked out the door.

"Heather?" He trailed behind me down the stairs.

Angel and Dante looked over at us. I didn't want anyone in our personal business, so I tried to walk to my car as quickly as possible.

Jared caught up to me and pulled my arm.

I snatched it away roughly. "I'm done! Leave me alone!"

"Fine. Go ahead and leave, then," he said. "Be done. Lose my number."

"Gladly." I continued to my car, got in, and left.

As soon as I got home, I put two scoops of chocolate ice cream in a bowl. Ice cream always made me feel a little better. Just as I was taking a first spoonful of the ice cream, I heard a few knocks on my door. I went over, looked through the peephole, and was surprised to see Dante standing there. Did he follow me home?

I opened the door, with a confused look on my face.

He backed away from the door with his hands up. "I apologize for following you, but I had to make sure that you were okay."

"That's kind of weird. Do you always follow people to their houses?"

He shook his head, with a nervous smile on his face. "No, not at all. Now that I'm standing here, I'm kind of embarrassed."

I was still frowning at him as I asked, "You and Angel moving?"

"I'm not moving, but she is."

"Oh . . . You guys broke up?"

"Yeah. It's a wrap."

"Why you break up?" I asked, curious to see if he knew she had been cheating on him.

"Come on. We both know why."

I continued to stare at him. Not only was he fine as hell, but he smelled good too. I could smell his cologne, despite the distance between us. Angel was stupid for cheating on him.

"You're home alone?" he asked, peering behind me.

"Why you want to know?" My guard was still up. And he might've been cute, but he was nosy as hell.

"I'm sorry. I shouldn't have asked you that. I'm going through a tough time with this breakup right now. I don't have much time to process it all, because soon I'll be back on the road, working."

"What do you do?"

"I'm a musician. I play the keys for various artists on tour."

"Really? You're a piano player? I thought you might've been a professional basketball player because of your height."

He laughed a cute little laugh as he showed his incredible smile. "I hoop, but not on a professional level. I've been playing the piano since I could talk."

"How long do you stay gone on tour?"

"Sometimes I'm gone for half the year at a time, with a few breaks in between. The other half of the year I spend rehearsing. I told myself that I didn't want to be in a relationship, because I feel like I'm married to my music, but Angel was persistent. She used to travel with me, but she hated living on the road because it limited her freedom. I didn't blame her. In the back of my mind, I knew she was seeing someone else, but I didn't expect it to be your boyfriend."

I sighed and shook my head. "How do you feel about that?"

"I'm crushed. How about you?"

"Hurt beyond measure." I tried not to think about how hurt I was feeling, but I couldn't help myself. "Jared knew what kind of relationship I came from before him. For him to do the same thing hurts, you know. I never expected this from him, of all people."

"I understand that feeling. We have that in common. Well, I just wanted to check on you. I'll let you get back to your day."

"Thanks."

"No problem. Have a nice evening," he told me before he stepped away from my door.

"You too," I called.

He walked toward his car. I closed the door and went to the kitchen to eat my ice cream, thinking about how crazy he was with his fine self.

Chapter 17

Troi

After hearing my baby's heartbeat for the first time, I felt elated. My desire to nurture this child was slowly building inside me. This baby was inviting me to be the best version of myself, to start over, to cast away the pessimism, and to make the loving nest that my inner self had been searching for. I was now looking forward to being a mommy more than ever. Rocko was just as excited because he had never heard any of his other children's heartbeat through a sonogram before.

"That was so amazing," he commented and smiled widely as we walked out of the office.

"That was *everything*," I replied, staring at the ultrasound pictures. "Thanks for meeting me up here."

"I'm glad you invited me to come. I almost cried up in there. Grown-ass man getting all emotional and shit."

I laughed at him. "I thought it was sweet of you to get emotional. Your heart isn't all the way cold."

"My heart isn't cold at all. That's just what you think. Is there anything that you need before I head to the house?"

"No. Thanks for asking, though." I placed the ultrasound pictures in the envelope the nurse had given me. "I'm going to head home."

"Okay. I'll call you later."

"Okay."

I liked when we got along. This co-parenting thing seemed like it was going to be a successful venture. Rocko was giving me the space I needed to heal my broken heart.

Chapter 18

Mai

I knocked on Heather's front door. It was a Wednesday, and Rocko came for Niara on Friday nights, but I couldn't find Rocko anywhere. He hadn't been answering my calls, so I had driven to San Francisco to see if this was where he was hiding. I had my driver's license, but he had had one of his homies deliver the car to me. I had expected Rocko to do it himself, and I wanted him to tell me about Troi's pregnancy.

Heather came to the door in a pair of ripped, hip-hugging jeans and a white tank top that showed off her stomach. Rocko wasn't lying about her weight loss. Homegirl looked good, but I couldn't help but feel a little jealous over her dramatic weight loss and toned body. Her short, curly crop fit her perfectly. I mean, she was still a simple bitch, but I liked her improvements.

"Mai, what you doing here?" she asked after she opened the door and sized me up.

"Is Rocko here?" I questioned, trying to look into her house.

"No. He won't be here until Friday night. Why? Did he tell you he was here?"

"No, but I can't find him anywhere in Sacramento . . ." I paused to see if maybe she was lying to me.

I didn't like being in the dark. He had been acting so weird, and I wanted a more detailed explanation about the money, the condo, and the car. I was beginning to think everything he had said to me was something he had made up to keep me out of the way.

"Do you know that Troi is pregnant?" I asked.

"Yeah, he told me, but I don't get in his business like that."

"What? He told you, but he couldn't tell me?"

"If he didn't tell you, how'd you find out?"

"I saw her at the clinic." I was the last one to know. I sucked my teeth, feeling even more irritated. "Can I come in and use your phone? Mine died on the way here, and I left my charger at home."

Heather opened the door wider so I could walk in. We walked up the stairs to her living room and kitchen area. I took a quick glance around to see if any of Rocko's belongings were lying around. Nothing but toddler toys, books, papers, pens, and highlighters were scattered about. Niara was playing with her dolls while watching *The Little Mermaid.*

"Excuse the mess. I'm in the middle of studying." Heather handed me her cell.

I dialed Rocko's number. He answered immediately, something he never did for me. "What's good?" he asked.

"Oh, so at least I know you know how to pick up the phone for Heather. This is—"

"Mai? What the fuck you doing at Heather's?"

"I wouldn't be here if you didn't avoid me. Why haven't you called me back? When you going to come see your son? I had to come all the way to San Francisco to try to find you, and I still can't find you."

"Go back home. I'll see my son this weekend, like I already told you." He hung up in my face.

I fumed, feeling as if I wanted to scream. "He makes me so sick. Why he always gotta treat me like a stepchild? I'm going to go home. Thanks, girl, for letting me use your phone." I walked back down the stairs.

"All right. Have a safe drive," she called after me.

"Bye." I walked out the door and sighed.

I guessed I was going to have to wait until Rocko was ready to deal with me. I was over this bullshit. I jumped in my car and got back on the freeway. From then on, I decided, I would do me. I wasn't going to flag down Rocko anymore.

Chapter 19

Heather

When was Mai going to get enough of chasing Rocko around when he didn't want her? He didn't want to be bothered with her childishness, and I didn't blame him. She was in her feelings all because she had found out about him having a baby with Troi. That was what her visit had been about. Unfortunately, Troi wasn't going anywhere, so I didn't know why Mai was still trying to interfere.

I was hungry, and it was well past my lunchtime. All that studying had me feeling famished.

"Niara, grab your shoes, sweetie. Let's go get something to eat. What you want to eat?"

"Chicken!"

"Okay. Let's go to Popeyes."

Niara put on her shoes, and so did I. I grabbed my keys, and we left the apartment. Popeyes was only a block away, so we walked. As we walked through the shopping plaza, toward Popeyes, a car pulled into the stall in front of the Safeway grocery store. I smiled when I saw Dante getting out of the car. He didn't see us, as he started walking toward the store entrance.

"Dante," I called.

He turned to see who was calling his name. "Oh snap. Look who it is," he said. "What y'all doing?"

"Heading to Popeyes for some lunch. You about to do some grocery shopping?"

"No, actually, I'm grabbing a sandwich from the deli and a Starbucks coffee."

"What kind of coffee you usually get?" I questioned.

"Caramel macchiato with soy milk and extra caramel."

"For real? That's my favorite, made the same way," I said.

"The same exact way? Isn't that something?" he replied with a huge, beautiful white grin.

"It is . . . Dante, I want you to meet my daughter, Niara. Niara, this is Mr. Dante."

"Hi, Mr. Dante," she said and waved.

"Hello, Niara. Well, aren't you gorgeous, like your mother," he said.

"Thank you," Niara said.

I felt flattered by his statement and grateful for the recognition. "You come to this Safeway often?"

"Pretty often," he replied. "I don't like going to the one by my spot. They don't make the sandwiches quite as well as they do here. How about I buy you guys lunch? I can roll to Popeyes real quick with you."

"Oh, no. That's nice of you, though. I don't want you to go through any trouble. We're fine."

"It's no trouble." He shrugged.

I smiled, feeling myself blush. "Not today." I didn't want Niara asking any questions about this man, and the thought crossed my mind to get to know Dante a little better. "You free this weekend?"

I couldn't believe that question came out of my mouth. Did I just ask this man out on a date?

He bit his lower lip as he nodded. "Sounds good. I'm free. You mind if I have your number?"

"I don't mind." I handed him my phone so he could save his number.

"I'll give you a call. Guess what?" he said.

"What?"

"I don't have to go on tour for another six months. The artist is pushing the tour back."

"Really? What are you going to do for six months?"

"Maybe I'll go on a vacation, but I want to buy a house, so maybe house hunting."

"House hunting will definitely keep you busy."

He smiled. "I like to keep busy."

"Nothing wrong with that. Where do you want to go for a vacation?"

"I still don't know yet."

"I'm so busy with school. I wish I could go on a vacation. Send me a postcard or a souvenir or something."

"I got you. So, what are you studying in school?"

"Criminal justice."

He raised his eyebrows. "So, you want to be a lawyer?"

"I'm going to be a lawyer."

He smiled widely. "Look at you. Are you almost done with school?"

"This is my last year, and then I'm off to law school."

"Sweet. Well, this weekend I'll take you to one of my favorite spots. It's called Stackz."

"Never heard of it. They got good food?"

"Oh, man, it's so good. I think you'll like it. Have you talked to Jared by any chance?"

"No. Why?"

"No reason. I haven't seen him in a few days, and Angel is MIA. I don't want to give it too much thought, but they could be together. Anyway, I need to move on. You working things out with him?"

"Oh no. That chapter is done."

He stared at me as if he were staring through me. "You're such an intelligent, beautiful, and well-put-together woman. Jared is seriously tripping."

I felt warm all over as I replied, "Thank you."

"Your little one is so quiet. Is she always like this?"

"Mostly . . . You have any kids?"

He looked at me as if that question had caught him off guard. "Um, yeah, I have a son."

"You do?"

"Yeah, but he and his mother moved out of the country. I haven't been able to locate them."

"How old is he?"

"He's five years old now." He went through his phone and showed me a picture of him.

"He's such a good-looking kid. How old is he in this picture?"

"One."

"He's so cute. What's his name?"

"Naiim. I want to see him again."

"I bet. Is there anything you can do?"

"Not when I don't know where she is. I'm on the verge of giving up. I hope Naiim will grow up strong and come looking for me when he gets old enough."

"I understand. I pray that you find him soon."

"Thanks. I'm going to let you and Niara enjoy the rest of your day and get your Popeyes. I'll call you."

"Okay."

"Bye, Niara." He waved at her.

"Bye, Mr. Dante."

He chuckled at her cute voice as he walked into the store and we walked toward Popeyes.

"Mommy?"

"Yeah?" I asked, still feeling giddy inside.

"Can I get some fries with my chicken?"

"You sure can, sweetie."

I was doing my best to move on and not think about Jared. But I wasn't trying to date anyone or see anyone so soon. Nonetheless, there was something about Dante that intrigued me. My mama had always said that the best way to get over a man was to get a new man, but that had never been my style. Still, it felt good to be flirted with by such a nice-looking guy.

Chapter 20

Mai

Cipher sat on my bed in the *forbidden* condo. *Fuck Rocko!* Since he couldn't answer any of my calls, and he was having another baby, I was going to do whatever I wanted. I liked Cipher's dick so much that I wasn't going to leave him alone. He had handled Neiosha like he'd said he would, and I hadn't seen her or heard from her.

"I see you doing your thing, baby. You got a new car, new crib," he said as he moved a blunt across the lighter to seal it. "What you do? Win the Lotto?"

I sat on the bed next to him, wearing nothing but a matching pink bra and panties. "You already know who my baby dad is, don't you?"

A small smirk appeared on his face. "I heard that today the police picked up his boy in San Francisco to question him about the murder of my cousin. Took them fuckers long enough to finish this investigation. It'll only be a matter of time before they get your baby daddy for killing my cousin."

My body stiffened. "Rocko didn't kill your cousin, Cipher."

"You really think he's going to tell you the truth?"

I didn't like hearsay, and I never believed anyone else's hype. I especially didn't pay attention to trash talking about Rocko, but he had been acting strange, and what if what Cipher was saying was true? I bet that was the reason why Rocko had had me hide that money, had given me that brand-new car and the condo. He was up to something, and I wished he had told me what it was so I could've at least known what was true or not.

"I don't know," I admitted. "He lies about everything."

He puffed on the blunt and then passed it to me. "Rocko is a straight sucka, and he's going to get what's coming to him. Believe that."

I took two puffs and passed the blunt back. I hopped up and put on some music.

Cipher watched me shake and move my ass seductively to the beat. He gave me a head nod to come to him. A naughty grin appeared on his face as I walked back to the bed. He lay back, placed his hands behind his head, and waited for me to straddle him. I sat on top of him and wrapped the bottom of my feet around his thighs.

"Take that sexy shit off," he demanded.

I loved his bossy swagger, and he had me going crazy. I looked down at him as the partial gold grill on his bottom teeth gleamed. Damn, he was sexy. He slapped my ass in anticipation of seeing me naked. Every time I stripped for him, his eyes danced all over my body, as if it was the first time he had ever seen me.

As soon as I was completely naked, he licked his lips and pulled my arm. He wanted me to give him some head, and I was more than happy to grant his silent request. I unbuckled his pants, took his thickness into my mouth, and worked him like a pro. He groaned on contact and grabbed the back of my head to touch the back of my throat. He loved it when I took it all without difficulty.

When he had enough, he pulled me up to get on top of him. My movements became liquid as I flowed on top of him. He took hold of my ass and helped me bounce faster and faster, until he busted.

I lay on top of him, feeling high from the weed. Our quick session was over. He moved me off him. Then he got up, pull up his pants, and reached for his jacket.

"Are you leaving already?" I asked with an attitude. "You just got here."

"I got moves to make."

"Can I come with you?"

He looked uneasy but then replied, "Come on. Hurry up."

We cruised around the dark streets of Oak Park in his yellow Thunderbird. I sat back and enjoyed the ride. I hadn't been out this way in a while, and it felt good to be baby free. I hadn't even noticed that we were on Neiosha's block until we stopped in front of her house.

What kind of messy shit was this?

He sensed my tension and said calmly, "Chill for a minute. I'll be right back."

Though I nodded, I was uncomfortable, because I wasn't trying to see Neiosha. I locked the car doors to help me feel a little bit better. It would've helped if it wasn't so damn dark outside.

Minutes later a few hard knocks on my window startled me. I looked up to see Neiosha glaring at me. She was wearing an oversize black hooded sweatshirt, so at first, I didn't know who she was.

Though she wasn't smiling, she said in a fake friendly tone, "Hey, girl. Roll down the window."

I shook my head.

Cipher walked up next to her and said to me, "Get out of the car."

Was he crazy? I shook my head again.

"It's all good. She's not tripping. Get out of the car. We all gotta talk," he told me.

I unlocked the door, but I clutched my purse in case I had to use my pepper spray. Cipher pulled the door open roughly before I could get all the way out.

"What's going on?" I asked.

"Cipher and I had a talk. I'm good with the two of you doing your thing," Neiosha announced.

They both laughed at the way I was staring at them.

I wasn't laughing. "Are you serious, or is this a joke?"

"Girl, ain't nobody gonna do anything to you." She smiled at Cipher. "Did you ask her about the money?"

Cipher replied, "Not yet."

"What money?" I asked, narrowing my eyes at her.

"Rocko owes me money, and I need you to help me get it back," he said.

"How the fuck can I help you get it back?"

"He's your baby daddy, so that's going to be up to you to figure out. All you have to do is ask him to hand it over," he replied.

"How much does he owe you, and when did you let him borrow it?"

"Oh, he didn't borrow it. The night he killed my cousin, he stole fifty thousand dollars from me."

My heart raced. I hoped it wasn't the money he had given me to put up.

"Something tells me that you know how we can get the money." Neiosha looked at me with suspicion.

I didn't know what to say or do. The last thing I wanted was be in the middle of whatever mess Rocko had created.

"I know where he keeps some of his money."

"You do?" Cipher asked, raising his eyebrow.

"It's in my closet at the condo," I revealed.

"You gone give it to me?"

"Yeah." I swallowed the hard lump that was forming in my throat.

"That's my girl. Let's go," Cipher said.

Rocko was going to kill me, because he had told me not to touch his money, but I didn't know what else to do.

Chapter 21

Troi

Before I could start my day at work, my cell rang. It was a blocked number calling. I almost thought of sending the call to voicemail, but something told me to answer it.

"Hello?" I asked.

"You have a collect call from the Sacramento County Jail from . . . Rocko. Press one if you would like to accept this call. Otherwise, please hang up."

What was his ass doing in jail? Anger filled me at once. I hoped he hadn't done anything stupid to that young baby mama of his. I hesitated, stared into space for a split second before pressing one. After a few clicks, he was on the line.

"Troi."

"Rocko? Why are you in jail?"

"I forgot my probation officer was coming by the house the other day, so he put a warrant out for my arrest. I turned myself in this morning, but can you post bail? I need to get out of here."

I blew air from my lips. "I can't do that."

"Why can't you?"

"I don't have much in my savings."

"It's only a thousand," he said.

"I know, and I don't have it."

"Can you please call Mai for me, then?"

I shook my head. He had the nerve to mention her name to me.

"Why didn't you call her in the first place?" I snapped.

"Look, I don't have a lot of time to talk. Will you call her on three-way, please?"

"Uh-uh, I'm not doing that."

"Dial the number, Troi. She has the bail money, because I gave it to her."

I was irritated, and I wanted him to know I wasn't pleased with his absurd request, but I followed his directions, anyway. I wrote down the number he gave me, and then I merged the call.

She picked up after a few rings. "Hello?"

"Mai," Rocko said.

"Rocko? What the fuck you want?"

I rolled my eyes. I couldn't stand the sound of her voice.

"I'm in jail. I need you to bail me out."

She made a disapproving sound with her mouth as she sucked her teeth.

A male voice in her background asked, "Who's that?"

"Nobody," she replied and then hung up.

"Hello? Hello?" Rocko said.

"I think she hung up on you," I said.

"Who the fuck was that?" he muttered, fuming.

"Hell if I know."

"Babes, you gotta help me out. I'll get you the money. Just get me out of here."

"Fine. I'll see what I can do."

"You know I'm a man of my word. When I say I got the money, you know I got the money. Call the bail bondsman right now."

"I will."

I hung up. Damn it. This nigga.

***

I sat in my car and waited for Rocko's release. It took about two hours before his bail was processed. He exited the jail, and I honked the horn. He jogged toward my car.

"Thank you," he said as soon as he got inside.

"Where am I taking you?"

"To your house."

I frowned and shook my head. "I thought we were going to get the money. Where's your car?"

"At home. I had Pop drop me off when I turned myself in. Take me to Mai's. I gotta get that money from her." He bit the inside of his cheek and clenched his teeth. He didn't like that he had heard some nigga on Mai's end of the phone call.

"Are you going to be cool? I mean, I'm not going to take you over there if you're going to start shit, Rocko."

"I need to go get this money, so I don't have to hear your fucking mouth about paying you back. Plus, I moved her into her own spot, and I gave her direct instructions not to let anyone over there, especially that nigga she been fucking with."

"You need to let that girl live her life. You're acting like you're her daddy or somebody."

He shot me this look that pierced me as he clenched his teeth. "As long as she keeps putting my son in danger, I'm her fucking daddy."

"Oh, wow. Where you move her to?" I asked.

"Elk Grove."

"What? I know you didn't move her to the complex we were looking at, did you?"

He shrugged his shoulders and replied, "You don't want to get married, remember?"

The pit of my stomach did somersaults. He was unbelievable. I didn't say anything else to him while I drove over to what was now Mai's place. We stayed silent the entire ride. Before long, we pulled up into the gated community, and I parked.

I turned off the car and rolled down the windows. It had taken us an entire year to find this gated community, and I loved it. How could he just give her my dream?

He got out of the car, headed up the small walkway, and knocked on the door.

Mai snatched the door open and yelled, "What the fuck you doing here?"

"Bitch, why you hang up on me? You got this nigga over here?"

She pushed him to stop him from walking inside. "Ain't nobody here."

"I don't have time to stand here and argue with you. I see the nigga's car right there. Give me my money."

"Oh, you're talking about the money you stole from him?" she asked with a smirk.

"What? Is that what that nigga told you? Get my money so I can roll."

"I gave it to him because you owed it to him. Now, get the hell on."

Rocko clenched his teeth and balled up his fist. He looked as if he wanted to pound on her.

I shifted in my seat nervously. Rocko had a temper, but I had never seen him put his hands on a woman before.

"Since you can't seem to follow directions, bring me the keys to my car, and I want you the fuck out of my house by the end of the day," he snarled.

She disappeared into the house, and he walked toward my car. He sat on the hood, looking as if he was ready to hurt the world.

She came out of the condo with a black duffel bag in her hand. "I'll be gone by morning. Take your stupid car. I don't need it, anyway." She dropped the duffel bag at his feet and tossed the keys on top of it.

He picked the bag up and shook it. "You really gave that nigga my money? Tell this bitch-ass nigga to bring his ass outside right now. Since he got a problem with me."

"No. I'm not telling him shit. That wasn't your money, Rocko, and you know it."

"You believe him over me? Yeah, okay. You'll see. I'll be back to get my son this weekend."

"Over my dead body. Looks like you'll be right back in prison once they find out you killed Greg Young, anyway, so you better worry about that," she told him.

Who was Greg Young? The name sounded familiar.

"Whatever," he said and then spit on the sidewalk. He placed his right hand underneath his shirt, then laid it on his stomach. Rocko smirked and shook his head. "I can't believe this shit."

Mai smiled and said, "I'll get out your house. Leave me alone after this. Worry about not spending the rest of your life in prison."

She walked away and went inside the condo.

Rocko stood there for a moment, clutching the duffel bag tightly.

"What was that about?" I asked as I leaned my head out the car window.

"Fuck her."

"What you about to do now?"

"I have money stashed in another place. I'll get it for you. I'm driving this car back to your place."

"Are you really going to make her move out of here?"

"Fuck yeah."

"You are something else. You okay?"

"I'm good. It's nothing."

"Don't act like that was nothing, Rocko. Why don't you tell me what's really going on? Who's Greg Young?"

"One day I'll tell you everything. Not right now, though."

"I think you should go to your mom's. This is too much for me."

He rubbed his face before blowing out a breath. He replied calmly, "This is serious, Troi. I can't trust Mai anymore, and I certainly don't trust the nigga she fucking with, so I'm going to your house."

The frown on his face remained as he stared at me and waited for my reply. He wasn't going to take no for an answer, and that was exactly what I was afraid of.

"Are you sure there isn't somewhere else you can go?" I whined.

"Quit trying to get rid of me, Troi. I'm not going anywhere but to your spot. So, cut that shit out, and let's go. I'll follow you."

I didn't know what was going on, but the tone of Rocko's voice had me saying, "Okay, okay."

Chapter 22

Mai

Rocko wasn't there for me when I needed him, so I had no reason to do what he wanted me to do. I had been Rocko's puppet for far too long.

"Rocko will get what he deserves. Niggas don't get away with the shit he's gotten away with," Cipher said as he paced the living room. "You lucky I didn't go out there and blow his brains out for calling me out."

"He's gone now, and you got the money back. Why you still worried about him?"

"This is bigger than the money, Mai. The police don't have to worry about solving this shit anymore, because I got this. I'm the only nigga who gives a fuck about my cousin."

"Do you really have enough evidence that proves Rocko killed your cousin?"

"I have all the evidence I need."

"Yeah? What's that?"

"Don't worry about it."

I rolled my eyes. I was getting tired of talking about Rocko. "Now that I don't have a car and he wants me out of here, can you take me to my mom's? I gotta pick up my son, anyway."

"I have a better idea. You and li'l man can stay with me, 'cause I know you don't want your mama all up in your business."

"Really? We can stay with you?"

"Yeah. I got a new spot in Lemon Hill. You'll love it."

Lemon Hill was on the other side of Elder Creek, which wasn't too far from Oak Park, but it was an Asian community. Well-known Asian gangs ran that neighborhood. It was too dangerous, even for my black ass.

"Lemon Hill?" I scowled.

"Yeah. You either down with me or you're not. If you ain't down, then we might as well be over. You down?"

I thought about it. I wanted to be down with whatever Cipher was down with.

"I'm with it."

"Good. Let's go pick up your baby, and then we'll head to the house."

I walked around the house with the baby in my arms. It wasn't what I had expected. Rocko's luxury condo had me spoiled. This was nothing but a raggedy-ass shack. It was empty besides one tiny love seat, a refrigerator, a table and chair, and a little-ass twin bed in one of the two bedrooms. Who did he think was going to sleep on that piece of shit? The house was filthy.

I thought he said this was a new house, I said to myself.

It felt so cold inside this house, and the lights didn't even work. He had battery-operated camping lanterns all over the place.

I guessed my face must've shown how disgusted I was, because he asked, "Why you looking like that?"

"Like what?"

"You looking like you're not feeling this."

"I'm not feeling this. Look at this dump. You expect me and my baby to stay here? You could've at least gotten the SMUD and PG&E turned on—"

Pow!

He backhanded me so hard that I saw stars. I should've fallen, but somehow I was still standing, with my son in my arms. As I tasted my own blood in my mouth, I was speechless.

"I ain't Rocko, so all that yapping you do to him don't fly with me. You'll like whatever the fuck I give you, ungrateful bitch. I don't give a fuck about what you like and don't like. That smart-ass mouth of yours will get you fucked up fucking with me." He left the house and slammed the door.

I could hear him locking the door from the outside. That was when I noticed there was no way to unlock the door from the inside. I went to the window and discovered it was covered with bars. I hadn't paid attention to any of that when we first pulled up. I had hardly paid attention to the address. I went to all the windows and saw that every single one was covered in bars. The front door was the only way out, from what I could see, and he had locked it. Did he trap me?

I placed the baby in his carrier, and he started crying. I needed to make my son a bottle. I tried to make the water hot in the kitchen sink, but it remained cold.

"What the fuck?" I muttered, fuming.

The small cut on the inside of my cheek hurt when I ran my tongue along it.

I was glad I had packed enough formula and diapers, or else we were going to be shit out of luck. Where was my phone? I checked my purse and the diaper bag. Nothing. Where the fuck was my cell phone?

Chapter 23

Heather

Rocko sent me a text saying he wouldn't be able to get Niara for the weekend, without any explanation. I thought of something rude to text as a response, but I erased it. I needed to hear his voice, so I could tell if he would tell me some bullshit. I always knew when he was lying. I called his cell.

"Hello," Rocko answered after a few rings.

"Why aren't you coming to get Niara this weekend?"

There was a slight pause from him before he replied, "There's some shit going on, but I should be able to get her next weekend."

I blew air from my lips. "What kind of shit?"

"I just got out of jail, because I missed my PO stopping by. I'm at Troi's right now. I promise once I get things settled, I'll come get her."

"Damn it."

"What? You had plans or something?"

"Yes. I'm used to you picking her up every weekend, so I made plans."

"I'm sorry, Heather. Can your mom watch her?"

I sucked my teeth. "Of course, she can, but I don't want her to ask me about what plans I have. It's private."

"I understand. You hear from Jared?" he said, prying.

"Nope. I told you I'm done with Jared."

"Listen, if you bring her to me tonight, I'll keep her for the weekend."

"You sure?"

"Yeah, but I have to check with Troi first. Is that cool?"

I had heard him when he said that was where he was, but I didn't think he would be there for the entire weekend. If he was going to be with Troi, then I would have to be okay with my baby being around her.

"I'm okay with it if Troi is."

"Hold on a second." He talked in the background to Troi briefly before coming back to the phone. "She said it's cool. Are you gonna come tonight?"

"Yeah. We'll be hitting the freeway in a bit. Send me her address."

"I will. Listen to me . . . I got word that the SFPD took Jared to the station for questioning about Greg."

"What? I thought that case was closed. Jared had already been questioned before, so why were they questioning him again?"

"They reopened the case."

"Really? Has anything changed since then or something?"

"I don't know."

I had always thought about what really happened to Greg, but when the case had closed, I had let it go.

"Damn. I hope they solve it. I just don't want them harassing you guys again."

"I don't want that, either," he said.

"Niara and I are going to get ready to head out in a bit."

"Okay."

I paused before saying, "I'm worried about you. I want all of this to be over so you can go about your life."

"Me too. You keep praying for me."

"I'll never stop doing that."

"Thank you. I'm texting the address right now."

Chapter 24

Mai

The baby and I fell asleep on that thin mattress in the bedroom. That was all we could really do. There was no TV and nothing to keep me entertained. Cipher took his sweet time getting back to the house. Hours went by. Suddenly, Cipher was on top of me, trying to take my jeans off. I looked up at him through blurred vision. He sloppily kissed my lips. His liquored-up breath covered my hands as I tried to push him off.

"Cipher—"

"Shut the fuck up, bitch. You know you like it when I give it to you rough. Isn't that what you told me?" He removed my pants.

"Cipher! Stop!" I tried to move his hands, but he was stronger than me.

"What?" he asked with a frown on his face as he entered my tight, dry hole. "You want this dick to fuck the shit out of you, remember? Didn't you tell me you love this dick?"

It burned like hell, as I could feel him ripping me.

I screamed at the top of my lungs, "Stop!"

He slapped me, not once or twice, but three times, left to right, and then to the left again. "Shut the fuck up and give me my pussy."

I couldn't believe that he was raping me. He put his hand over my mouth to muffle my screams. By then, my son had woken up and was crying. That didn't stop Cipher. He drilled me hard until he came deep inside of me. As soon as he was done, I curled up into the fetal position.

"Now get your ass cleaned up and take care of that crying, punk-ass son of yours before I cut his li'l head off." He stomped out of the room and slammed the door behind him.

I was scared for my life and my son's life, so I quickly put my pants back on and held my son close to my heart. "Shhh, baby. It's okay."

Tears poured from me as I sobbed silently.

Once the baby was quiet, I placed him back on the bed, in a comfortable position. I stood on my shaking legs. I wanted my phone, but I was too afraid to ask him if he had it. I carried the camp light from the bedroom to the bathroom to get some tissue for my bloody nose. On my way, I had to pass the living room. Cipher was smoking a blunt, with Neiosha sitting on his lap, while his other homeboy rolled another blunt. I hadn't known other people were in the house. Had Neiosha heard me screaming? I couldn't believe that she would sit there and listen to me cry like that without helping me.

Neiosha smirked slyly as we made eye contact. This was payback, and she was enjoying every moment of it.

"Did I tell you to come out of that fucking room?" Cipher barked at me.

"No. I—"

"You what?" he snarled.

"I need to use the bathroom."

"Hurry up and get back in that room."

I rushed to the bathroom and quickly wiped my nose and peed. I left the bathroom, and as I passed the living room, I said reluctantly, "Am I going to school tomorrow? If so, I need to take the baby to my mom's tonight."

"You ain't leaving this house," Cipher muttered.

"But I have to go to school."

"That's out."

Too afraid to argue with him and get hit again, I lowered my head and asked, "Do you have my cell phone?"

He cocked his head to the side. "Don't ever question me, bitch. Do what the fuck I tell you to do, and get your ass back in that room."

Neiosha laughed, as if this was the funniest thing she had ever witnessed.

I had no phone, no food, no hot water, and no way of getting out of the house once the front door was locked. I felt like a prisoner. "Cipher, I'm hungry."

He pushed Neiosha off his lap and hopped up. Neiosha stood next to him. I backed away toward the wall, afraid he was going to charge at me. "I'll bring you back something. Come on, y'all," he said instead.

He walked out, and they followed him. He locked the door.

My whole body shook as I cried. I hadn't cried so hard in my life. My chest felt tight, as if I couldn't breathe. As hot tears streamed down my face, I felt like a complete fool. I looked around the house to see if there were any other ways of getting out, but there weren't. I panicked and started hyperventilating. All sorts of evil, twisted things ran through my mind. *I wish I had listened to Rocko.*

When Cipher returned, it was hours later. I was sitting on the love seat, my baby next to me. Cipher came back with food, to my surprise. He tossed the bag into my lap. I didn't like how he threw the bag at me, but I didn't dare complain. This nigga was crazy as fuck. My already swollen face would hate me for talking recklessly, so I said nothing. I was starving, so I ate. He watched me intently while I finished the fried chicken meal. Suddenly, I felt so strange and woozy.

I held my head. "What the fuck? Nigga, did you poison me?"

He laughed with an evil glare and said, "I don't know how Rocko can stand dealing with you and your mouth."

He grabbed me roughly, picked up some rope he had on the table, and tied my hands to the back of the chair. My feet were next to be bound to the chair. I looked over at my baby. He was sleeping, snuggled up in a blanket on the tiny love seat.

Cipher put a strip of duct tape over my mouth before he stepped outside. The whole time he was out there, I couldn't help but try to figure out his next move, but the drug he had slipped me had my head rolling around. He returned with a gas can and started pouring gas all over the place.

"I can't believe how easy you have made this for me." He laughed. "My plan has gone smoother than I thought it would. I never thought you would sweat me so hard. You claim you love Rocko, but nah, you don't. What woman would help her man get set up like this? You gave up the cash and the ass without having to kick your ass for it. Now you and your punk-ass son are going to burn in this fire."

He tossed every bit of gas onto the floor before he walked over to the front door, laughing. After dropping a lit match at the end of the trail of gasoline, he walked out and locked the door behind him. Black smoke quickly engulfed the room, and it didn't take long before I started having a coughing fit. With my mouth taped shut, it was even more difficult to breathe. Through the smoke, I couldn't see my baby, but I could hear him crying. The glass in the windows burst from the blazing fire.

Suddenly, someone kicked in the front door. I couldn't make out a figure through the smoke, but this person grabbed my baby and ran out of the house with him.

When the person returned, I heard, "Mai, Mai . . . Hold on! I'm trying to get to you, but the fire is everywhere."

Neiosha covered her face with her arm to shield herself from the blaze.

Chapter 25

Troi

Rocko was eating his favorite take-out Chinese food from Rose Garden. The way he was gulping that cola to wash down his mouthfuls had me staring at him. He seemed fidgety and nervous. More drama was brewing; I could feel it. Whatever Rocko had going on made him antsy, something I had rarely seen in him.

"I called my mom and told her I was here," he said. "She can't wait to see Niara tomorrow."

"That's good. I'm sure she's going to enjoy her."

"Are you sure it's okay for Heather to drop off Niara?" he asked with his eyebrows raised. "I mean, if you feel uncomfortable, I completely understand."

I shrugged and replied, "It's fine, Rocko."

He nodded his head as he took another forkful of chicken chow mein.

"I got some things I really want to talk to you about," I said. "Can I ask you something?"

He looked up from his plate, frowned, and replied, "Depends on what you going to ask." It was like him to answer like a smart-ass.

"Rocko, we've never had a heart-to-heart about many things concerning your personal life without you lying. I'm hoping you can tell me the truth now."

His eyes softened while he leaned back in the dining chair. He burped. "Excuse me." He hit his chest a few times before drinking his soda. "What's on your mind, beautiful?"

"If you still want to marry me, like you say, then I have to know *everything* about your past relationships. I want to talk about your other baby mamas."

He studied me for a moment, and I could see the internal debate he was having with himself, but I gave him a stern look. I wanted him to give it to me straight.

"All right. I'll tell you whatever you want to know," he said.

"From the beginning, and you better not lie to me ever again about anything."

"I promise."

"Okay, so let's start with Heather. How'd you meet?"

"You gonna get mad if I tell you?"

I rolled my eyes. "I won't get mad. I want to know the story."

"I'm quite sure you're about to get mad. You always get mad, and then I would be putting my business out there for nothing. What you want to know this shit for?" He shoveled more food into his mouth.

"Because I need to know. It's like I need a better understanding of why they are the way they are with you, and why you are the way you are with them. Are you going to tell me or not?"

He folded his arms. He didn't start speaking again until all the food in his mouth was chewed and swallowed. "I met Heather on the first day of school when we started high school, so, like, ninth grade. She was a chubby, short thing, but she was fly. She was always up on the fashion tip and had this long hair that went past her bra strap. Skinny bitches were jealous of her because even though she was chubby, every boy liked her. She was tough, had to be, since she was raised in the Sunnydale projects like me. I stepped to her 'cause I could tell she had a thing for me. She smiled whenever I was near. Heather was so down for me off the top, day one. She did whatever I wanted her to do. When she got pregnant, I tried to do right by her, but I was in the streets hard. I had to move to Sacramento to get away from the heat in San Francisco, and then I met you, and you know the rest."

"Why didn't you tell me you had a baby on the way or even a girlfriend when we first met?"

"I wanted to impress you. I loved Heather, but there was something about you. I didn't want to hurt her feelings or yours, and I couldn't tell either of you what the deal was. Even though she had been so down for me, I wanted to be with you. She was having my baby, but I didn't want to miss the opportunity with you."

"Did you ever question whether your daughter was yours or something? Because I don't see how you didn't say one word to me."

"Heather was a good girl. She didn't get down like that. She was too madly in love to see anyone else."

I hesitated before I asked, "Do you still love Heather?"

"Am I in love with her? No. But I'll always have love for Heather. She's my first. We're in a good place now."

"Good. Now, about Mai. Why'd you even go there with her when we were still together?"

"I ask myself that question every single day. Mai is one of them loudmouthed broads, you know, a bitch who thinks she can have any nigga she wants. She was only sixteen when she first walked up to my car and asked me to take her and her friend to the mall. No matter how much she flirted with me, I didn't give her the time of day. It wasn't until she was almost nineteen, and you and I had been fighting tough. That's no excuse, but I used that to fuck around with her. She lied about being on birth control. That was my fault. Now she's my worst nightmare."

"Do you love her?"

"I never loved her. I care about her because she's the mother of my son, but I don't love her. She's like a rebellious child." He got up from the table and wrapped his arms around my waist. "You and I, though . . . I fell in love with you at first sight, and I've made major mistakes in our relationship, but I know how to fix it to where we can be brand new all over again, if you let me. This time, I won't lie. I won't cheat. I won't play any games."

"What if you go to prison? Then what? Your children will be hugging their daddy from behind bars. That's not a fair life for them."

"I'm not going back to prison or jail, not if I can help it."

"Can I ask you something else?"

"Go right ahead."

"Were you there when that kid Greg Young was shot?"

I stared into his eyes, and he stared right back at me without blinking. His expression didn't even change.

After I had heard Mai mention Greg Young's name, I had Googled him. He was murdered a couple of years ago, and the case had never been solved.

Just then, there was a knock on the front door.

"Are you expecting company?" he asked, looking as if he was relieved that he didn't have to answer that question.

"No." I frowned, wondering who was at the door.

"I should've brought my gun," he said, removing his hands from my waist.

"What? That's not necessary. It's probably Heather, with Niara," I said.

"Not that fast. She won't be here for another thirty minutes."

I went to the front door, but he gently pushed me to the side so he could look through the peephole first.

"It's my mom," he said, opening the door, with confusion all over his face. "Hey, Mama. What you doing here?"

"Is there anywhere we can go and talk, Rocko?" she asked in a trembly voice.

"You guys can talk in the kitchen," I said.

I led the way and motioned for her to sit at the table.

As soon as she sat, Rocko questioned, "What's going on?"

She seemed hesitant, as if she couldn't find a way to say what needed to be said.

"I can go in the bedroom, so you two can talk," I said.

"No, sweetie," she said. "You should hear this."

My heart started beating faster as I sat across from her.

"The police came to my house, and they're looking for you, son."

Rocko groaned, as if nothing was new. "What they want now?"

"Something terrible happened to Mai."

Immediately, his body got real stiff. "Something terrible like what?"

Tears appeared in her eyes as she took a deep breath.

My already drumming heart started beating harder, and the pit of my stomach was filling with fear. Rocko's body stiffened as he stared at his mother.

"Mai was killed in a house fire tonight."

"What? Where? Her mama's house?" he quizzed, frantic.

I gasped and covered my mouth with my hand.

She shook her head slowly. "No. She was in some abandoned house off Lemon Hill. Someone called the police when they saw the house on fire. They found her burned body bound to a chair. The police came to my house, and they need you to go down to the station."

Rocko groaned again. "Are you serious?"

"Yes, son."

"Why they want to question me? I wasn't anywhere near Lemon Hill today."

"The police were acting like they think you're a suspect or something, without coming out and saying it. When's the last time you seen her?"

"Earlier today I went by the condo I put her and my son in. I've been with Troi since then. Mom, where's my son?"

"No one knows. The police are looking for him."

"Mai didn't leave him with her mom?" he asked.

"No. Her mother doesn't know where he is."

Rocko covered his face. "No. This can't be happening."

"This is crazy," I said. "Rocko, you have an alibi tonight, so you'll be fine if you go talk to the police."

"I'm not going anywhere near the police station. Them fuckers will try to twist shit, like they always do. I gotta find my son."

"You know where to find him?" his mama inquired.

There was another knock on the door. I jumped a little, because it startled me. Rocko and I stared at one another, and I prayed it wasn't the police. I started to get up, but Rocko put his hand up.

"I'll get the door," he said. He went to the door and stared out the peephole. "It's Pop." He opened the door for him.

"You hear about the fire?" Rocko's father asked as he stepped inside.

"Yeah, Mama just got here and told us."

They walked into the kitchen.

"Hey, Roy," Rocko's mother said.

"Hey, Mint," Rocko's father answered.

Chapter 26

Rocko

There was no question in my mind as to who was behind this. Mai hadn't let me in the house because Cipher had been in there, and I had called him out. He hadn't liked that shit. He already had it out for me because he thought I killed his cousin, a theory people kept running with, which was ridiculous. This was why I had told Mai to stay away from him. Cipher was the worst kind of nigga to know. He was ruthless, but he had been underestimating the kind of nigga I was.

"I'm going to find my son before that bitch-ass nigga does something else he'll regret," I said.

Troi's wide eyes searched mine. "Who?"

"Cipher, the nigga Mai was fucking with. He was in the house when we went over there. I gotta go find my son." I grabbed my keys from the counter.

"You're not going alone," Pop said. "I got your back."

I nodded. "Okay, cool. Let's roll."

"Wait," Troi said. "How do you know where to look?"

"We're going to check every spot we know," I answered.

I gave Troi a kiss on her lips and Mama a kiss on her cheek. My kisses weren't going to be my final goodbye, so they didn't have anything to worry about.

"I love you, Mama. I love you, Troi. Lock this door, and do not let anyone in. I'll be back."

Pop and I left the house.

"I'll drive," I said.

"All right. Go to Fourth Ave first. I usually spot his T-Bird that way."

Heather called me as soon as I started up Mai's car. I had forgotten that she was on her way with Niara.

"Hey, Heather," I answered and connected her call through Bluetooth.

"I'm about fifteen minutes away, but Jared just called and wanted to know if you can meet up with him. He wouldn't tell me why."

I sighed heavily. "Meet up with him for what?"

"He didn't say why, but he sounded weird."

"I'll call him and see what he wants," I replied. "When you get over to Troi's, I need you and baby girl to stay there until I tell you to leave. I have to do something really fast. I know you have plans, but some crazy shit is going on right now. Don't answer any calls from anybody other than me. Don't even answer Jared."

"What? Why? You got me bringing your daughter to you, and you're not even there?"

"Listen to me, Heather. You need to stay at Troi's tonight. Can you do that for me?"

"Oh, my God, Rocko. What are you talking about? I'm not staying at that woman's house."

"Yes, you are. Mai is dead, and my son is missing." I got choked up as a tear slid down my cheek.

She got silent.

"Did you hear me, Heather?"

"I heard you, but what do you mean, Mai's dead? What happened?"

"I think Cipher may have set her on fire."

"What?"

"Yeah, so you and Niara need to hurry up and get here. Stay at Troi's."

"So, you expect me to stay with Troi in her house after what she did to me?"

"Look, I need you to put aside that childish beef. This is serious business, Heather. Can't you hear how serious I am right now?"

I could hear the panic in her voice when she replied, "Oh my God! Do you think Cipher would try to come after us?"

"I don't know, but I need you to calm down, Heather . . . Heather?"

She was breathing real hard. "Yeah?"

"Get to Troi's as fast as you can. Did you tell Jared where you were going?"

"Well, I told him I was coming to Sac to bring Niara to you, but I didn't say where."

"Text me his number, please."

"Yeah. Sending now."

"All right. Drive safely."

"Okay, I will."

I hung up, and Pop said, "I got a funny feeling about Jared. Him and Cipher still tight?"

"I don't know. Cipher been in Sac, and Jared been in Frisco. No telling, though."

"Call him. Let's see if he knows where we can find li'l man."

I got the text from Heather, so I called him.

"Hello," Jared answered.

"This Rocko. You wanted me to call you?"

"You good?" he asked, as if we were cool all of a sudden.

"What you mean?" I asked.

"The pigs had me at the station and shit about Greg. They hit you too?"

"Nah. You been in contact with Cipher?"

"Me and that dude ain't been on talking terms for a while now. Why?"

"I'm looking for the nigga."

"For what?"

"I need to holler at him."

"Nah, I haven't talked to him. Heather and Niara get there yet?"

"They're on their way."

He sighed heavily into the phone. "This shit ain't cool anymore."

"It's been not cool. You might need to protect yourself, because I'm not sure what Cipher is up to."

"You think he tripping?" Jared asked.

"He most definitely is."

"Damn, man. I wanted to see if you would meet up with me."

"Meet you where?" I raised my eyebrow.

"At the port, near Pier Seven."

"Pier Seven? I'm not going anywhere near that place, especially since . . ." I paused, shaking off the bad memory of the night Greg was murdered.

"Well, then, just meet me at my spot."

"I need your address. Text it to me."

"A'ight." I ended the call and headed toward the freeway.

"You want to go all the way to San Francisco right now? We gotta find Junior," Pop reminded me.

"What if he has Junior?"

"You think that's why he wants to link up?"

I shrugged. "Could be. Might be worth the drive."

"He said the police was questioning him, right?"

"Yeah," I replied.

"What if he's wired?"

"Damn. You think he might be?"

"You never know. I got a funny-ass feeling in my stomach, son. You strapped?"

I didn't have a gun on me, but I remembered there was a 9 mm in the glove box. I reached over and pulled down the lid to the glove box. My gun was still hidden in the corner.

I pointed. "Got one right here. You strapped?"

He pulled up his shirt and showed me his gun. "I stay strapped."

Chapter 27

Heather

On my way over to Troi's, I cried. I couldn't help it, because Mai didn't deserve to die, and I prayed her son was all right. I didn't really know how to feel about staying at Troi's house, but as uncomfortable as I was, I was going to squash my issues with her.

As soon as Troi opened her front door, I wished I wasn't standing there holding Niara while she was sleeping. I never thought we would have to come face-to-face ever again.

Surprisingly, her face was soft as she smiled. "Come in."

Her smile could've been real, but I wasn't sure. I preferred a fake-ass smile over a frown any day. I carried Niara inside. Troi bolted the door and secured the place behind me.

"What an impressive alarm system," I said. "Doesn't surprise me. Rocko has gotten himself in enough trouble over the years. It's probably needed."

"He made sure my place had the best security system. Get comfortable. He says you may be here awhile." Troi led me into the living room.

Rocko's mother was sleeping peacefully on the couch, with a blanket draped over her.

"Thank you. Where can I put her? She is getting heavy."

"Um, actually, you can put her in my bed. Go upstairs, and it's the last door straight back. Would you like me to get you some wine, soda, or water?"

"You have anything stronger? My nerves are all over the place."

She nodded as if she understood where I was coming from. "I have a little minibar that I can no longer enjoy for a while. I would drink with you if I could . . . Um, will Grey Goose do?"

"Perfect." I headed up the stairs, noticing all the up-scale décor. The paintings, the vases, the Spanish tile on her floor . . . This was the way Rocko liked his women to live.

I laid Niara on Troi's queen-size pillow-top bed and covered her with the comforter. Troi's bedroom was decked out. Her bedroom furniture put my little bed-room stuff to shame. I wasn't sure if it was Rocko's influence or her own. After admiring the decor, I tiptoed out and made my way back down the stairs. I took a deep breath before meeting Troi in her kitchen, where she had my shot of vodka on the granite counter.

"I'm not sure if you need some juice or if you want it straight," she said.

"I'll take it straight." I downed the shot quickly.

She nodded slowly. "You want another?"

"One more for now, but don't take that bottle too far away."

She poured more, and after I downed that shot, she motioned for me to take a seat at the table. She sat down across from me and stared at me, though I noticed she was trying not to stare too hard. This was the first time she had taken a good look at me.

"I'm sorry if I'm staring at you," she said. "It's just that you're really beautiful."

"Thank you. You are too." My hands were shaking, and I clasped them to try to calm them. "I'm so shaken up over what Rocko told me about Mai, I don't know what to do. I mean, I couldn't stand Mai, but damn, why her?"

"I know, right? This shit is crazy. Rocko is so heartbroken. I hope they find the little guy. He's such a precious baby."

"Yes, he is. I wonder why this is all happening right now. The whole Greg Young murder thing just won't go away."

"Today was the first I've ever heard about Greg. He's never talked about him. Were they friends?"

I nodded. "They were closer than close. Rocko was like his big brother."

"So, what happened? Trying to get Rocko to talk about things is like trying to pull teeth. He's too secretive," Troi said.

"Tell me about it. All I know is that Rocko was there the night it happened, and it traumatized him. He told the police he wasn't there."

"Why would he tell the police he wasn't there?"

"Street code," I said. "He doesn't want to be a witness, and he ain't a snitch. Jared even said he wasn't there, but I don't know. The two of them lie so much."

"Jared's your boyfriend, right?"

"Jared *was* my boyfriend before I caught him cheating. I've always felt like Rocko and Jared fell out over something bigger than me, you know. They've gotten themselves into some deep shit."

"Do you know anything about Cipher?" she questioned.

"I've never met him, but I've heard his name plenty of times. From what I have heard, he ain't a good dude."

"Rocko thinks he killed Mai."

"He told me that too."

There was silence between us. I listened to the house to see if Niara had got up. The house was perfectly quiet.

Troi broke the silence after a few moments. "I'm sorry about—"

I held my hand up. "It's in the past. You were hurt, and you acted out of anger, and I should accept that. You had no idea what was going on. Rocko is one hell of a liar, and he made a fool out of all of us."

"I know, but I wish I could rewind the hands of time and handle that situation differently."

"Apology accepted. We don't ever have to talk about it again. We don't have to fight. Are you and Rocko working things out?"

"God, I don't know. I can't help that I love him, but he is just . . . ugh."

"He loves you very much. He told me that, and I believe him. You have a way with him that I've never seen before," I admitted.

As she sat in front of me, Troi let a few tears fall from her eyes. "Do you think he'll come back to us alive?"

"All we can do is hope and pray." I lifted my glass for a refill, and she got up to retrieve the bottle.

As soon as the shot glass was filled, I took it to the head. Deep down, I was more than nervous. Things would be so different if he wasn't the father of our children. Rocko coming back to us alive wasn't solely about us. It was about our kids too.

Chapter 28

Rocko

I didn't pull into Jared's complex, because I didn't want him to see my dad in the car. I wanted him to think I had come alone, just in case I was walking into a setup.

"You sure you don't want me to go in with you?" Pop asked.

"Nah, stay here. If I'm not out in twenty to twenty-five minutes, come get me."

"I got you."

I looked around first before I got out of the car. I walked into Jared's apartment complex and looked for his apartment. When I saw that it was on the second floor, I jogged up the stairs. I looked around again before knocking on the door.

Jared let me in and closed the door behind me as soon as I was inside. I glanced around the apartment before I sat on the couch. Jared remained standing.

"Did Heather and Niara make it?" he asked. "I've been trying to call her, but she's not answering." He looked worried.

"They're good."

Jared took a drink from the fifth of Hennessy that was on the coffee table. "You want some?"

"Nah, I'm good."

"More for me." He took another gulp before screwing the top back on. "You want to tell me what else is going on?"

I wasn't going to tell him what had happened to Mai, so instead I asked, "What the fuck the police ask you?"

"The same questions they already asked. It's like they trying to catch me in a lie or something, but I haven't lied about shit. I wasn't there when Greg got killed."

I nodded and watched him pace the floor. I paid close attention to his shaking hands. He seemed nervous about something. It crossed my mind that he knew all about what had happened with Mai and my son. "You said you haven't been in touch with Cipher, right?"

I had to ask him again to see if he would switch it up. Over the phone was one thing, but to see Jared's expression was another.

"You already asked me that. Look, after Greg was killed, I stayed out the way. What's up with you and Cipher? Y'all beefing?"

"Something like that . . . You and me beefing?" I said, giving him a hard glare.

"You tell me." He sipped his Henn again.

"Nah, I'm straight. We grew up like family, nigga. You should've never got at Heather behind my back, though."

"Whatever. You didn't want her." Jared hummed lowly to himself and seemed lost in deep thought for a few seconds.

"What?" I asked in an effort to break his train of thought.

"You know, your story about what happened to Greg has never added up."

"You got amnesia or something? Now you sound like the police."

"Who killed him?"

"It wasn't me."

"If it wasn't you, then who was it?"

I leaned forward, with a scowl on my face. "The police got you wearing a wire or something?"

"The police will never have me wearing a wire. You can search me if you want."

"Then why you pacing like that?"

He stopped, and his expression conveyed that he hadn't realized he was pacing.

While I continued to stare at Jared, with a deep frown on my face, someone came out of the closet behind me and struck me on the back of my head with a hard object. I blacked out.

Chapter 29

Troi

Heather and I laughed so hard, our tummies ached. I had never thought she and I would connect and have so much in common. She was so fun to be around.

"I'm drunk," she said, laughing.

"Girl, you have me too weak right now," I said and laughed. I cracked up as she ran her fingers through her hair with her eyes closed. "You are fucked up. I'm jealous. I need to be fucked up with you."

After checking the security cameras for the third time, I felt my insides continue to do flips. We were laughing to keep ourselves from worrying.

"What you got to eat in here? I'm doing all this drinking and need to eat," Heather said.

"Rocko ordered all that Chinese food, so have at it."

Heather helped herself to the boxes sitting on the counter. "Honey walnut shrimp, yes. Hey, this goes to work right here. High five, Rocko."

"I think he got some house fried rice in there too. I have bowls in the cabinet to the right."

She grabbed a bowl and picked up one of the plastic forks from the counter. "I can honestly say that being with Jared and Rocko has taught me a lot about what I don't want in a man. I'm pissed that I can't have my lunch date with Dante tomorrow."

"Sounds like you were looking forward to it."

"I was. He's charming, he's handsome, and he's nothing like Jared or Rocko. Meaning he don't sell dope." Her cell phone rang. She took it out of her pocket and looked down at it and smiled. "Speaking of the devil. There goes Dante right now." She answered the call. "Hey, Dante." She walked out of the kitchen.

Every time I thought about Rocko, I felt pain in my stomach. The fact that Pop was with him was the only thing that made me feel a little bit better. I kept looking at the security cams to make sure no one was lurking around here. I had no idea what this Cipher looked like, and I wasn't trying to find out.

Chapter 30

Heather

"I had planned on being right back, but something crazy is going on with Niara's father," I confessed to Dante, slurring my words. "I won't be able to make our lunch date tomorrow. I'm sorry."

"Wait? Something crazy like what? Are you drunk?"

"I've . . . I've been drinking to get me through this bullshit."

"Get you through what bullshit? What's going on?"

I broke down and cried. Through my sobs, I said, "Rocko's son is missing, and his other baby mama was murdered. I'm trying to keep it together, but I can't. Wait, I shouldn't have said that. Forget I said that."

"Wait. What? Did you guys call the police?"

"The cops already went to his mother's house. That's how he found out about it."

"Heather, where are you? I can come to you."

"Nooo. Rocko said to stay at Troi's house and not let anyone in, but I'm so scared. I don't know what's going to happen next. My nerves are all over the place. Rocko's not here, and I don't know when he's coming back."

"Would you feel better if I came over there?"

"I would, but Rocko said to not let anyone in."

"Where is he?"

"He's out trying to find his son."

"Heather, I'm worried. This doesn't sound right. Does he know who would do this?"

I plopped down on Troi's couch. "He has a pretty good idea."

"Listen, I won't be able to sleep tonight, knowing that you're scared. If I can't physically see that you're okay, then I'm going to worry to death."

I sighed. "I wish you were here."

"I know you haven't known me for long, but what you're describing doesn't sound cool at all."

"It's not cool. Troi has a good security system, but the more she checks the cameras, the more nervous I get. I really want to see you right now."

"I'm putting on my shoes and getting my coat. Give me the address, and I'll be right there. I won't stay long at all. I just want to see you."

"Hold on. Let me check with Troi first." I stumbled back into the kitchen, and Troi was watching her monitors like a hawk. She snapped out of it when she realized I was there. "Hey, Dante wants to come by to make sure we're all right. I know Rocko said not to let anyone in, but I'm scared, and I want him here."

Troi looked nervous, and I could see that she was afraid as well. "To be honest, I'm freaking out myself. Tell him it's cool."

"Okay." I put my ear back to the phone. "She said it's fine. You sure you feel up to driving to Sacramento?"

"It's no problem. Shoot me the address via text, and I'll be right there."

"Okay. See you soon."

I hung up and sat down at the kitchen table, across from Troi. As I fumbled with my phone to send him the address, I couldn't help but notice the perplexed, anxious look on Troi's face.

"What's the matter?" I asked.

"Rocko or Pop hasn't called. I'm worried."

Chapter 31

Rocko

I woke up in Jared's empty bathtub. My hands were zip-tied in front of me. One eye was closed shut, and blood was dripping into the other. I looked down to see my shirt covered in blood from the back of my head. Blood was everywhere. Through the eye that wasn't swollen shut, I looked up to see Jared and Cipher glaring down at me. I should've known that this was a setup. These punk-ass niggas had taken turns beating me in and out of consciousness before putting my ass in the fucking tub. They would've never been able to handle me one-on-one. They had had to catch a nigga from the blind side.

Where was Pop? I wondered. He should've kicked in the door by now.

"Where's my son, bitch?" I asked as I spat blood.

"His little ass burned with your baby mama," Cipher replied.

"Nah . . . he didn't. The police told my mama that someone saved him."

"Well, then, I guess that wasn't his destiny, now, was it?" Cipher said.

"What the fuck y'all doing this for?" I asked.

"You should've never crossed us, nigga," Jared said, with fire in his eyes.

"You started sleeping with my baby mama behind my back, and you want to talk about crossing somebody?" I countered.

"Don't make this about Heather, nigga. You didn't give a flying fuck about her. Think about why I hooked up with Heather in the first fucking place. It wasn't because I wanted to be with her. I wanted to know where the money was, but she didn't know shit," Jared seethed.

Cipher added, "You were supposed to kill Heather instead of playing Daddy and shit. Both y'all niggas soft when it comes to these bitches. You see, I ain't got no problem cutting a bitch off."

I said, "Heather didn't even know anything about the money."

"Oh, we figured that out. That was Jared's job to drop her ass a long time ago. He obviously failed at that mission. His ass fell in love with the bitch."

Jared cut his eyes at Cipher, shaking his head vigorously. "I didn't fall in love."

"Yeah, okay," Cipher scoffed.

"Why'd you have to kill my baby mama?" I muttered.

"You better be glad I didn't kill your whole family. I should've killed you a long time ago. Do you know how many times I crossed your path and been by your house? This worked out better for me, though. Getting to Mai was a piece of cake. I didn't have to persuade her. She threw that pussy at me the same way Heather did for Jared. Your women are weak as fuck. Maybe Troi would've been our best bet. She's your trophy bitch. You would've given up the money a lot sooner if we'd gone after her." Cipher cocked his gun and pointed it at me. "Tell me why you killed my cousin."

"I didn't kill your cousin. I didn't know any of the niggas that showed up on the pier that night."

"And yet you walked away unharmed, with all the dough, while my cousin got fucked up," Cipher snarled.

"Greg died because—"

"Because he was trying to protect your ass. He was always so loyal to you for no fucking reason. I still don't get it."

"Greg had my back, but where the fuck were y'all? Huh? I had to pay Queen, or else we would be dead too. Did you ever thank me for that?"

"Thank you for what? You must be crazy," Jared replied.

My chest heaved up and down as I swallowed hard. They had a hell of a plan to make me feel the wrath. "You two never showed the fuck up—"

"Nigga, we had the wrong fucking address, because you switched up at the last minute," Cipher said.

"I didn't switch up shit." Anger coursed through my whole body. "Y'all want to trip over fifty Gs? Y'all niggas are stupid."

"What was supposed to be ours was supposed to be ours. You didn't have to kill Greg, but you did," Cipher yelled.

"That night . . ." I paused to stop myself from talking about it, but then I determined that it was time to let these dumb niggas know the truth. "Greg called me after you two bozos never showed up. He stressed that I should pick him up, and you want to know what he said? He said that you two had purposely left me hanging."

Cipher gritted his teeth. "Your ass is lying. My cousin would never say no shit like that."

"You mad because he was more loyal to me than you?" I shot back.

Cipher hit me with the butt of the gun, and I blacked out. The night of Greg's murder played like a film in my mind.

*Jared and Cipher were supposed to meet me under-
neath the light-rail station so we could meet Queen
at the pier to cop some cocaine. I had told them that I
would front the money and we would split up the dope.
We each had our own hoods to run, but we weren't quite
kingpins yet. Jared was running shit in Fillmore. Cipher
had Oak Park. I ran Meadowview in Sacramento. That
deal was supposed to be our way of supporting one
another to hustle harder. When they didn't show, Greg
called me, and I picked him up.*

*Greg was one of those young niggas who didn't finish
high school and wasn't going to. He was smart and
should've had his head in the books somewhere, but
there was no convincing him to return to school. The
streets had him. When he told me that Cipher and Jared
was on some shady shit, I was pissed, but I wasn't going
to let them stop me from finishing business with Queen.*

"Thanks for rolling with me, nigga," I said.

"You know it's no problem. Cipher's my cousin, but
that nigga is a snake. Straight up. I don't like the way
he moves. You should've had me on the job with you,
anyway."

"I wasn't about to involve you. You should be studying
in school."

"Nah, I'm studying these streets, and my best bet is to
learn from you, 'cause you're the best to do it," he said
as he threw his cigarette out the cracked window. "I
wouldn't even tell you nothing crazy, and I for damned
sure would never do my cousin in, but . . ."

"But what?"

"Cipher and Jared ain't acting cool right now. You
sure you can trust coming to the pier after they stood
you up?"

"I've been dealing with Queen since I was in high
school. She's cool." I kept my eyes on the road. Once I
came to a red light and stopped, I looked over at him.

He lit a Black & Mild cigar. "If some shit pop off, I gotta bust somebody's ass."

"I appreciate that, but it's good. I'll hand her the fifty racks, and boom, she'll hand me the shit. Easy. Fast. No problem, and we're gone."

"I hear you, but just in case."

"Since you're down for me, I'll front you some work out of it," I told him.

"Hell yeah. I'm ready."

"A'ight."

We arrived at Pier 7 close to midnight, as agreed. Dadiana Chacon, aka Queen, was a Mexican drug cartel leader who smuggled cocaine from Colombia. Once she moved to the Bay Area, I was introduced to her. The transactions I made with her always went smooth.

Greg and I walked along the planks and were greeted by a group of five men. All the times I had met up with Queen, she had never been this deep. She usually brought only one or two guys, so that large group raised a red flag.

"Where's Queen?" I asked, looking around.

An unfamiliar face replied, "Queen sent us. She couldn't make it." He nodded his head toward another tall guy.

The guy came over to me and started searching me.

I held my hands up. "We ain't strapped."

He searched Greg next. The tall one gave the leader a head nod to let him know we were cool.

"You got the money?" the leader questioned.

"Of course I got the money." I held up the bag. "You got what I came for?"

He gave a head nod to a nigga with a big duffel bag. "Someone called Queen and said something about you trying to short her, so we're her protection plan, but if you say it's all there, then it's good. Let me tell her you made it."

I frowned. Who would call and say some stupid shit like that?

He called her from his cell. "He's here . . . Yup." He offered me the phone.

I took it from him and said, "Queen?"

Her Spanish accent was thick as she answered, "You have my money?"

"Yeah, right here. What's going on? I thought I was meeting up with you."

"Nasty things are getting back to me about you. I'm just making sure you come correct."

"I've been knowing you since I was sixteen years old. I know how you get down. I got all your money."

"I had to make sure."

"You never have to worry about me not holding up my end of the fucking deal, Queen. I'm a man of my word."

"Good." She ended the call.

I handed the phone back to her little messenger. "Hey, give me what the fuck I need, so I can leave." I was irritated. "You can check it out if you need to count it."

"I said we're good. Now turn around and walk away."

"Wait. Hold up. Where's my dope?"

"You ain't getting shit. Turn your ass around and walk away."

The five niggas drew their guns on us.

I scowled and looked over at Greg. This was that bullshit. They were going to take the money without giving up the coke.

"I'm not leaving without what I came for. So, Queen is just gonna rob me like this?" I growled.

"Nah, nigga. This us. We keeping the dope and the money," the leader replied.

Fuck. If Queen didn't get her money, I was good as dead. I turned to walk toward the car, trying to think of a way to make up for the loss. I thought Greg was walking with me, but I suddenly realized he was not at my side. Then shots were fired.

When I turned to locate Greg, I saw him running away. He had snatched the bag of money. I dashed after him, and more shots ripped the air. They missed us as we ran all the way down the pier to the car. As soon as we were inside the car, I sped off. They shot out the back window, but we managed to escape.

When I looked over, Greg was taking deep breaths, and he had his hand on his stomach, where blood was oozing out. He was dying right there in my front seat. I tried to get him to the hospital as fast as I could, but it was too late. He died before we could get there.

Cipher slapped me. "Wake up, nigga."

I realized I was still in Jared's bathtub. I looked up at Cipher. "If you didn't try to get over on me and Queen, your cousin would still be alive. He had my back and wasn't about to let those niggas rob us. So, in essence, you killed your own cousin."

"Fuck you. My cousin wasn't supposed to be there. It would've worked perfectly. I told Queen that my niggas would make sure they handled you when you got there."

"You left out the part where you told them to take the money and the dope, leaving me and Queen high and dry. I had to pay her off to make it right, because at the end of the day, I introduced you. You're lucky she ain't kill us."

"You know what? I'm sick of hearing your mouth." Cipher cocked his gun and put it to the side of my head.

I looked him in his eye, daring him to shoot me. If it was my time to go, then it was my time to go.

Cipher turned and shot Jared in the head instead. Jared dropped to the white-tiled floor as his brain matter splattered on the walls.

"That nigga was too weak over pussy to be on my team. Now it's your turn," Cipher snarled.

Boom!

The front door was kicked down. I hoped it was my dad and not the police. I hadn't been able to figure out what was taking Pop so long. I hoped some shit hadn't gone down outside.

Cipher walked out of the bathroom. After a few seconds, I heard gunshots.

I was breathing hard, watching the bathroom door to see who would walk in. With each second, my heart felt like it was about to beat out of my chest. Suddenly Pop entered the bathroom, and I heaved a sigh of relief.

"What took you so fucking long? Cut this off," I said, holding up my hands.

He took a knife out of his pocket, cut the zip tie, and helped me out of the tub. Pop put his fingers to his lips to tell me to be quiet and not to say another word. We walked out of the apartment and down the stairs.

Once we were in the parking lot, he said, "I don't trust talking in there."

"What took you so long?"

"Some niggas rolled up on me outside. I had to let them know who the fuck I was."

"You kill them?"

"Nah. Scared them away, some li'l niggas. I was walking up to the door when I heard the gun go off. You killed Jared?"

"How could I do that with my hands tied like that? I was almost a goner. Fuck. How am I going to find my son now?"

"We'll find him if we have to knock on every door in Oak Park."

My cell phone was ringing, and I pulled it out of my pocket, but I couldn't see who was calling, because my vision was blurred. "Hey, Pop, can you tell who's calling?"

He leaned over and took a look. "Says unknown. We gotta roll. The cops will have this place surrounded any minute now."

I answered the call as we walked to the car. "Hello?"

"Rocko, this is Neiosha."

I frowned. "Neiosha? Mai's friend?"

She hesitated a minute before she said, "Yeah. Um, I have your son. I'm trying to get him to Mai's mom, but I think she's at work or something."

I heaved a sigh of relief. "You have my son? Is he all right?"

"I can't get him to stop crying. Took me forever to get your number. I was scared to take him to the police because I don't want Cipher to do anything to me."

"You don't have to worry about Cipher. I'll get my son from you. I'm in San Francisco, though, but I'm on my way. Where can I meet you?"

"On Broadway, at Foods Co. How long will it take you?"

"Make him a bottle to soothe him if you can, and I'll be there in about an hour."

"I can go to the store and get him some milk. Shit, I don't know what to buy. Similac stuff?"

"Yeah, and I'll pay you back when I get there."

"Cool. I tried to save Mai too, but the fire was . . ." She started crying.

"Neiosha, don't cry. Thank you for trying to save her. Everything is going to be okay. I'll meet you in about an hour."

"Okay." She sniffled.

I hung up, and it felt like I could breathe again. We got to my car, and I tossed Pop my keys. Sirens were wailing in the distance.

Chapter 32

Rocko

When Pop pulled up alongside Neiosha's car, she looked the same way she had sounded over the phone, scared out of her mind. Her eyes were wide, and tears were streaming down her face. My son was wailing as she tried to rock him. Poor girl didn't know how to soothe him. I got out, opened her car door, and got my son from her.

She handed me the milk and bottle she had bought. I gave her forty bucks.

"Rocko, are you all right? You're bleeding." Neiosha frowned.

"Yeah, I'm good. Hey, thanks for taking care of him."

"No problem. What do I do now? Cipher is going to kill me when he finds out what I did."

"No, he won't, 'cause he's dead."

She lowered her head and replied, "What he did to Mai was fucked up, and I feel so bad. By the time I tried to help, it was too late."

"Mai wouldn't listen to me."

"I know. What if the police come by, asking questions about Mai? What am I supposed to tell them?"

"If the police come around, tell them that you rescued my son from that fire. You can tell them you know for a fact that Cipher did it, but that's up to you," I suggested.

She drew in a deep breath. "I owe it to Mai to do the right thing. God, I'm so mad at myself right now. I let petty shit come between us. Cipher played my ass too. I had no idea he was going to do that to her."

"At least you tried to make it right. It might've been too late, but at least you tried."

She nodded slowly as she stepped out of her car. She went to her trunk. She pulled out an olive-green army duffel bag and handed it to me.

"I think this belongs to you."

I frowned. "What's this?"

"Cipher gave it to me to hold until he came back from the bay."

I opened it up and saw that it contained the money that I had given Mai. "Thanks."

"You're welcome."

I watched her get into her car and back out of the stall in the grocery store parking lot. I got in the back seat of Mai's car, and Junior stopped crying. I didn't have a car seat to put him in, so I held him while Pop drove us to the house.

"We got him," Pop said.

"Yeah."

We were silent for the rest of the ride.

As soon as he pulled up into Troi's driveway, I noticed an H3 parked along the curb, but no one was inside it.

"Who's car is that?" Pop asked.

"I have no idea." Holding Junior, I got out of the car and walked toward the H3.

Troi came running outside. She must've been watching on the security camera. She dashed over to me.

"Oh, my God, Rocko . . ." She paused as she stared at my beat-up face; then she looked at the baby. "You found him."

"Whose car is that?" I said.

She placed both hands on my cheeks. "What in the hell happened to you?"

"Troi, is someone else in the house?"

"Yeah. Heather's friend Dante. Why?"

"What? I told Heather not to tell anybody she was here."

Troi narrowed her eyes at me. "He came because he was worried about her. He said he was going to stay until you made it back. We felt better with a man over here."

"What the fuck did she tell him to have him so fucking worried? I specifically told her not to tell anyone!"

"Calm down. Everything is all right, but you don't look good at all. What happened?"

I stepped real close to her, so she could hear me loud and clear. These hardheaded broads were getting on my damned nerves. "Do you see my face? I almost died tonight. Mai is dead, Jared is dead, and Cipher is dead. You and Heather over here are taking this shit too lightly. Y'all like to do whatever the fuck you want to do. When I tell you to do something, you got to do it the way I say to do it!"

"I know, but we were afraid, Rocko."

"Man, watch out." I gently pushed her out of my way so I could go back to the car.

"Rocko, I—"

Pop interrupted, "Rock, I'm gone go ahead and get out of Dodge."

"No problem. Thanks for being there for me."

"No thanks needed. Try to get some ice, medication, and rest. Night, Troi."

"Night, Pop," Troi replied as she walked over to me.

Pop went to his car, got in, and drove away.

"Where's my mama?" I asked, glaring down at Troi.

"Inside. She's asleep, and Niara is in my bed."

We headed to the front door, and as soon as we were inside, I locked the door and secured the place back up.

I laid my son on the couch in the living room, making sure there were enough pillows so he wouldn't roll off. I sighed, sat down beside him, and covered my face with my hands.

"I'll go get you some ice," Troi said, heading to the kitchen.

Heather walked into the living room and said, "Thank God, you're back. Where you find the baby?"

I growled, "Why the fuck you got some nigga up in here? I specifically told you not to tell anyone where you were."

She looked at me as if I was crazy. "Dante cares about me, and he wanted to make sure we were all okay. He drove all the way up here from San Francisco, and I don't care if you're mad about it. I'm glad he did."

"How long you been knowing the nigga?"

"Why?"

My head was pounding like crazy. I held the back of it. "Because of all that's been going on, I don't fucking trust nobody."

Dante walked up behind her and asked, "Is everything cool?"

I glared at the tall muthafucka. "We straight, so you can leave now."

"I'm Dante." He extended his hand out to me.

I wasn't shaking his hand. "I don't give a fuck who you are. Get out of my fiancée's house."

"Rocko," Heather said as her face turned red.

I didn't budge. It was my job to protect them, but these crazy-ass women in my life kept making stupid mistakes that kept putting my life in danger. I had a fucking plan. I always had a plan, but these bitches kept fucking it up.

"I'm not going to stand here and let you talk to him like that. You had a hell of a night, and it looks like you've got your ass handed to you, but don't take any of it out on him," Heather barked, taking Dante's hand to walk him to the door.

I stared at my son and thought about Mai. There wasn't anything I could do to bring her back. I was going to have to raise my son without her.

Troi brought me a bag of ice, Tylenol PM, and a tall glass of water.

"You have anything stronger, like a Perc or Vicodin?" I complained.

"Nope. This is it. You want me to drive you to the hospital?"

I gave her a look, as if to tell her, "Hell no."

Troi sighed and looked over at my son. "So, you're going to be able to tackle the single-father role with two kids for the entire weekend?"

"Single-father role? Why would I assume the single-father role when I'm not single?"

"Who are you with?" she asked, a confused expression on her face.

"Man, don't play with me right now. You already know what's up."

"When did we get back together?"

"You and I are going to spend the rest of our lives together," I stated matter-of-factly.

"Whoa. Slow down, patna, 'cause you're speeding."

"I thought we were working things out. We're having a baby, and we had our heart-to-heart talk. You asked me all the questions you wanted, and I answered."

She folded her arms across her chest but didn't respond. The look in her eyes told me that she wasn't feeling me anymore. Everything I had done was too much for her. Everything I had put her through was something I was going to have to carry on my own shoulders.

"I read you loud and clear, Troi. I'll always love you, though. Know that. Believe that."

"I hope you find yourself a woman that you'll have a fresh start with, and maybe you won't make the same mistakes again."

If she was done with me, then she was done with me. There was no need for anything else to be said.

"Okay, Troi."

"Your bedclothes are already in the bathroom."

"While I'm in the shower, can you keep an eye on my son?"

"Okay, I can do that for you."

It hurt to stand up, so I moved slowly. I looked at the front door to see if Heather was coming back in yet. I didn't see her. I turned to Troi and said, "Hey, I have a funny feeling."

"About?" she asked as she pulled the blanket up on Junior.

"I think Dante might be the police."

"What? Why you think that?"

"Something ain't right, and his posture ain't like niggas from the streets. Where she say she meet him?"

"His chick was fucking around with Jared. They were Jared's neighbors."

"His bitch was the one that was fucking with Jared?" I scowled.

"Yeah."

"Oh, well, he act like the police, riding all the way over here to play captain."

"You're just paranoid, Rocko. Go take a shower and get some sleep."

I couldn't explain why I was feeling the way I was feeling. I had been around all kinds of people, but there was something about Dante that wasn't sitting right with me.

Chapter 33

Dante

Heather's beauty had me captivated from the first time I laid eyes on her. No, I hadn't expected to flirt with her or her to flirt with me. It was killing me that I would have to look her in those beautiful eyes and tell her that Angel wasn't my ex-girlfriend but my partner, and her real name wasn't Angel but Antoinette.

Antoinette and I were undercover. Disguised as a couple, we had lived underneath Jared to gain his trust to obtain the evidence we needed for the Greg Young homicide. Antoinette was the type to do whatever—and I mean whatever—to bring someone down. She had thought that sleeping with Jared would get him to tell her everything she needed to know, but he had been so vague.

My real name was Dante, but I had never given Heather my last name. I hadn't had enough evidence to finally put Dadiana Chacon, aka Queen, away. We had thought Jared could lead us there, but he hadn't, and now we were banking on Rocko. He was the only one who knew everything about Queen and the truth about how Greg Young had died. We were almost there.

Heather was hugging me right outside Troi's front door, and I wanted to kiss her. Who knew that going undercover would result in such a great reward? I wanted her for real. That was the truth. I loved the way her head tilted back when she laughed. I loved how intelligent she was. Everything about this woman amazed me. If I wasn't a police officer and I met her out somewhere, I would've approached her.

"Thank you so much for coming to see about us," she said with her cute button nose scrunched up.

I caressed her hair. "It's no problem. I feel much better knowing that you ladies are safe."

She yawned and giggled. "I'm so sleepy. I drank entirely too much tonight."

I bit on my lower lip to fight the urge to kiss her. "You should get some rest."

"Yeah, I will. You don't know how happy I am to see Rocko back in one piece."

"He's definitely lucky."

My cell phone started vibrating in my pocket. I had a feeling it was the precinct calling to give me more details on my next move. There was no way I was going to be able to take this call with Heather near me.

"Hey, your phone is vibrating against me. Go ahead and take your call. I gotta go pee, but don't leave yet, because I want to give you a kiss." She went into the house.

I took the call. "Hello?" I answered.

"We need you to arrest Rocko Cooper right now," Antoinette said.

"Right now? For what?"

"You know that bug we had planted in Jared's house?"

"Yeah."

"We heard everything. Rocko is an accessory to the murder of Cipher, and they were talking about Queen. We can get him to talk."

I thought of Heather, Troi, and the children. It wasn't a good time to do this. "I can't do that at this moment."

"Well, a few officers and I are on our way to Troi Anderson's house," she said.

"No. Ask the captain if you guys can pick him up in the morning. I don't want to be here when you guys come."

"Why? Because you're screwing one of his baby mamas?"

"Antoinette, I'm not having sex with her."

"*Yet* anyway. They'll be there any minute." She hung up in my face.

"Fuck," I said under my breath. Just when I started walking away from the door toward my car, Heather came out of the house.

"You're about to leave without a kiss?" she asked.

Just then, the first squad car pulled up across the street, and the second arrived right behind it, both of their lights flashing.

"There's something I need to tell you," I said.

She looked past me at Thornton, Antoinette, and Rogers as they got out of the cars. They walked onto the lawn. I didn't make eye contact with any of them. I was pissed that they were doing this right at that moment.

"Can I help you?" Heather asked, gazing at Antoinette, a look of confusion on her face. I could see her mind trying to put the pieces together.

"We're looking for Rocko Cooper. Is he here?" Thornton questioned.

Heather didn't respond.

The front door opened, and Rocko appeared.

"Rocko Cooper?" Thornton called.

"Yeah," Rocko said.

"Put your hands behind your back. You're under arrest."

He didn't resist. He did what he was told. When they searched him, they found his gun.

"Why are you arresting him?" Troi questioned as she came out of the house.

"He's under arrest for the murder of Rod Stanley, aka Cipher," Antoinette replied. Then she addressed Rocko.

"You have the right to remain silent. Anything you say will be used against you in a court of law. You have the right to consult with an attorney."

As Antoinette walked him to her police car, Rocko said to Troi, "Call my lawyer."

Troi nodded.

Thornton patted me on the shoulder. "Detective Morgan, Captain wants you to give him a call."

I nodded at him and replied, "Sure thing."

As soon as my eyes met Heather's, it felt like my heart had dropped to my knees.

"Detective Morgan?" Heather asked, with a confused look. The immediate tears in her eyes as she stared through me rocked me to my core. "Isn't that Angel?"

"My name is Dante Morgan, and I'm an undercover detective for the Sacramento Police Department. My partner, Antoinette . . . Well, you know her as Angel. We were assigned to the Greg Young homicide."

"What?" Heather held her chest as her tears slid down the sides of her cheeks. "You're a cop? Angel is a cop?"

My heart was pounding, and I wanted so badly to lie, but the game was over. My heart sank further, like the Titanic, as I nodded.

"So, you're telling me that you used me to get to Rocko?"

"Heather, I—"

"No. Don't. You should leave."

"Please let me explain. Can we go inside and talk?"

"Fuck you." She stomped away and left me standing there with Troi.

Troi stared at me and snarled, "Rocko told me before he got in the shower that he thought you were a cop."

"Did he?"

"Yeah. You really think Rocko murdered Greg Young?"

"No. We know he didn't, but he was involved in the killing of Cipher tonight. Try to get some rest. I'll try my best to keep you posted."

She nodded slowly.

I walked inside the house and took one last look down the hall, hoping that Heather would reappear. I wanted so badly to walk in that bedroom and plead my case to Heather, but what she needed was some time. She already had a challenging time trusting men. I walked out of the house as the two police cars were driving away. Rocko was in the back seat of one of the cruisers.

The captain wanted Antoinette and me to do the questioning once I made it to the station. Antoinette was wearing blue slacks and a light blue button-up shirt. Her hair was pulled back in her usual bun, and she brandished her badge proudly. She always looked completely different when she wasn't undercover.

As soon as we sat at the table across from Rocko and his lawyer, I noticed Rocko was calm. I wondered if that was his poker face, to mask his true feelings. If he wasn't going to cooperate, he would spend the rest of his life in prison.

"I'm Detective Dante Morgan, and this is my partner, Detective Antoinette Jones. We were assigned to the Greg Young homicide a few years back. We have some questions we need to ask you."

Rocko was silent, but his lawyer spoke. "He doesn't have to answer anything. You have no grounds to keep him here. Uncuff him right now."

"We can't do that. Rocko will be charged as an accessory to murder if he doesn't cooperate. Who killed Cipher, Rocko? Who else was there tonight?"

"Don't answer that," the lawyer said to Rocko with narrowed eyes.

"We can make the accessory to murder charge go away if he gives us Queen," I stated.

Rocko chuckled. "So, that's what all this has been about? Y'all want me to help you get Queen?"

Rocko's lawyer grabbed his hand to stop him from talking. "My client isn't obligated to speak about matters that don't involve him."

"Oh, this very much involves him," I retorted.

"I'm sorry, but you have no grounds to hold him, and he doesn't need to answer any of your questions. He already told me what happened tonight, and it was self-defense."

"Self-defense? He was carrying an illegal firearm tonight, and it was loaded. Each bullet is some serious time. He's still on probation. We can put him back in jail on that alone," I reminded.

Rocko drew in a deep breath and said, "Was getting close to my daughter's mother part of your investigation? Dirty-ass cops always in too fucking deep."

I cleared my throat and looked him in the eye. I wanted him to leave Heather out of this. "Give us what we need on Queen, and you're free to go. Otherwise, you will face charges for the gun and for being an accessory to the murder of Cipher."

Chapter 34

Heather

All I could see in my head was Dante's smile. All I could hear was his laugh. He had felt so genuine, but he wasn't. *Everything* had been a complete lie.

I had locked myself in Troi's bathroom. I clutched my stomach and closed my eyes tight to stop the room from spinning.

"Heather, are you okay in there?" Troi knocked on the bathroom door.

Rocko's mother came down the hall. "Was that the police? Where's Rocko?"

I could hear them clearly through the door as I rested my back against it.

"They came and arrested him," Troi said. "Saying something about killing Cipher."

Rocko's mother sighed heavily and replied, "I was hoping he and his father wouldn't do anything stupid. They find the baby?"

"Yeah. He's sleeping on the couch. I don't know what to do right now. I'm shaking. I'm nauseous. I'm tired. How am I going to take care of his baby boy?"

"Don't worry about it, Troi. I'll look after my grandson."

Troi knocked on the bathroom door again. "Please, open up, Heather."

"What's wrong with Heather?"

"The guy she likes was working undercover to get to Rocko."

Rocko's mother groaned and spoke to the door. "Heather, come out, baby. We all gotta stick together on this. We're here for you."

I opened the door, with tears pouring down my face. They embraced me. I cried like a big baby. "I'm trying to make sense of it all," I said. "I don't remember what I may have said to Dante about Rocko . . . Oh, God . . ."

"I'm sure you didn't say anything to incriminate Rocko," his mother said.

"I'm reviewing everything in my mind to see if I said something that could hurt his case. I don't know what to think right now."

"We all don't know what to think right now," Rocko's mother said. "Our best bet is to stick together. I pray that Rocko won't go to prison for life. If he does, we gotta raise these babies the best we can. You gotta be strong for the children. You hear me?"

I nodded.

Chapter 35

Rocko

"May I please have a word with my client?" my lawyer asked the officers.

"Sure," Dante said. "We'll be back in five minutes."

The officers left me alone with my lawyer.

She asked, "You used to work for Queen?"

"Long, long-ass time ago. All my dealings with Queen have been over for years. Even if I knew where she was, I'm no snitch. The moment I rat is the moment I'm dead. Fuck witness protection. Should I just take the deal for having the gun?"

"If you take the deal, you'll be looking at five to fifteen years. You don't exactly have a clean record."

"I just want to post bail and go home."

"It doesn't look like that's going to happen unless you agree to help them out. The state will do everything in their power to pin all three murders on you if they can, but I won't let them do that."

This wasn't going to go away, but there was no way I wanted any piece of Queen. They were going to have to get her on their own. "If I give up Queen, you might as well plan my funeral now. I went to Jared's tonight only to talk to him to see if he had any information on my missing son. I had no idea Cipher was already there. They had me zip-tied in the bathtub, with a gun pressed to my head."

"You told me that already. Okay, listen, I'll fight for you."

My lawyer motioned at the window for the officers to come back into the room.

"What's it going to be, Rocko?" Dante asked.

"He can't help you get Queen, because he doesn't know where she is," my lawyer asserted.

"What if I told you *I* know where she is?" Antoinette said. "All you gotta do is meet up with her, get her to talk, and we'll get her."

"Y'all tripping," I said, folding my arms across my chest.

My lawyer grabbed my hand to stop me from talking. "If you know where she is, then you go get her," she said. "The only thing he's guilty of is carrying an unlicensed firearm."

"And he was an accessory to the murder of Cipher," Antoinette said.

"Well, you're just going to have to take it to trial, because he's not confessing to anything."

Dante looked defeated as he hung his head. They had no idea where Queen was, and there was no way in hell I was going to point them in her direction.

I was sentenced to two years in prison on gun-possession charges. That was the best my lawyer could do for me. I was grateful for that because I wound up serving only one year in Solano Prison, versus spending up to twenty-five years to life for the accessory-to-murder charges. There'd been no way I was going to give up my pop, but it hadn't mattered. Those charges had been dropped, by the grace of God. The recording they had couldn't be used in court.

Between my mother, Pop, Troi, and Heather, I was able to do my time in what seemed like no time. Heather brought Niara to see me every other weekend. My mom was able to get Junior to visit once a month. Though I missed the birth of my new baby girl, Tajsa, Troi was understanding and brought her to see me every weekend. She finally agreed to give us one more chance. It took me enrolling in programs and getting my welding certification for her to believe that I was moving differently. I didn't do it just to impress her; I did it for me. And so after one year, I walked out of prison a new man.

When I got out, Troi was right there waiting for me. I squeezed her tightly and said, "Damn. You looking good as fuck."

She smiled. "Thank you."

"Where's my baby?"

"She's in the car with your mom."

I smiled widely and reached for her hand. She held my hand as we walked through the parking lot.

"I'm ready to make love to you. I don't have to fantasize about it anymore," I told her.

"That makes both of us."

"Good." I pulled her to me and kissed her.

It felt good to be able to kiss her without the guards hovering over my shoulder, telling me to keep it short.

My mama yelled from the car, "Come on, y'all. I'm starving. I know you can't wait to eat some real food."

I hopped in the back seat with Tajsa, and I threw my lips to her little fingers. "Daddy's girl. What's Daddy's girl up to?"

It was no surprise that she looked a lot like Niara. All my kids looked like me and my mama. Tajsa grinned at me before sucking the juice out of her sippy cup.

"Anybody talk to Heather today?" I asked.

"I talked to her this morning," Troi answered. "She's bringing Niara tonight."

"Cool. Cool. I want to pick up Junior today too."

Silence fell over the car while my mama pulled out of the parking lot.

"What's up? Why you two get quiet?" I said.

Troi answered, "Mai's mom isn't going to let you see your son anymore. She also stated that she wants full custody."

"What? Why? She's been letting him come up here to see me. Why the sudden change?"

Troi shook her head. "I have no idea."

"She can't take my son, right?"

"You're going to have to go to court," Mama answered.

I sighed loudly and rubbed the top of my head. In my mind, I had figured that once I got out, I would have all my kids, and I could start planning out this wedding with Troi. The last thing I needed was for Mai's mother, Leslie, to bring more drama into my life.

Chapter 36

Heather

I drove across the Bay Bridge with the windows down, music pumping. Niara was in the back seat, nodding her head to the music. I could clear my mind of any kind of stress I had been going through. I had finished my last year at San Francisco State, and I had earned my bachelor's degree in criminal justice. Whenever I drove to Sacramento, I always thought about Dante. He had called me a few times, but I hadn't answered. My mom had even said that I was overreacting. She wanted me to give him a chance because, according to her, how we met didn't matter. I might've overreacted, but how else was I supposed to act? Dante was an undercover cop who was investigating my baby daddy. I felt he had used me to try to get information out of me. Dante had apologized a million times, and he had expressed that he had fallen for me, but was that real?

"Mommy, are we going to see Daddy?" The sound of Niara's voice brought me out of my daydream.

"Yes, baby, we're on our way right now."

"Is he out of jail?"

I cringed. I hated that she knew he'd been in jail. I wanted to hide it from her, but Rocko had insisted on telling her. He wanted her to know everything about him. They had grown closer while he was behind bars, and their bond warmed my heart.

"Yes, Niara."

"Yay. Do I get to see my sister and brother today too?"

"I think so. You eat your orange?"

"Yes, Mommy, I ate all my orange. I'm a little thirsty, though."

"You should have a bottle of water in that backpack."

"Oh, yeah. I'll get it."

I hummed while I tapped my fingers on the steering wheel. My cell phone rang. I turned down the music and answered using my radio.

"Hello?"

"Hey, Heather. It's me, Veronica."

"Hey, cousin. You find out anything?" I said, hoping she was able to help me dig into Dante's past.

My cousin Veronica was a private detective, and she had connections all over the world. I figured she would be the best person to find out things that nobody else could, especially about Dante.

"I located Dante's baby mother. Dante wasn't lying. They exist. It was a bit tricky to find her. I had to get in touch with so many people, but, anyway, I spoke with her."

"You did?"

"Yes, and listen, she didn't sound very happy about me finding her, but I explained how much Dante wanted to see their son."

"Why is she in hiding from him? Did he do something bad to her?" My heart felt like it stopped beating as I waited for her answer.

"No, nothing like that. She used to be the girlfriend of a mob boss. He had her seduce Dante to find out if he was undercover. She found out that Dante was a cop, but she had fallen in love with him by then, so she told her boyfriend that Dante wasn't a cop. She started working with Dante to bring down her boyfriend, the mob boss. Well, the mob boss found out and nearly killed her. She was able to escape and fled the country. She mentioned that she sent Dante a few pictures, but she never disclosed where she was."

"She didn't think Dante would keep her protected?"

"She felt like she had put Dante's life in too much danger already. She said it was easier to go away."

"Is she going to let Dante see his son?"

"She prefers to keep things this way and to stay out of his life. I'm sorry, Heather."

"No problem, cousin. Thanks for finding that out for me."

"I love you."

"I love you too."

I ended the call. I had verified that this part of Dante's life was real, but I felt sorry for him.

"You got your water?" I asked Niara.

"Yep. Turn the music back up."

I turned it back up as I pulled up into Troi's driveway. Before I could get out of my seat belt, Niara was running up to the door. She was so excited to see her dad. Troi answered the door, with Tajsa on her hip. It was really a trip to see how much Tajsa and Niara looked alike.

"Hey, Ni Ni," Troi greeted Niara.

"Hey, Miss Troi," she replied, running past her into the house.

I said, "She wants to see her daddy so bad."

"I know, right? It's all good. He can't wait to see her as well."

"Where's Rocko?"

"He's in the living room. Can't you hear him yelling?"

I heard him exclaim, "I need my son!"

"Who's he talking to?" I scowled.

"Mai's mother. She won't let him see Junior."

"Why not?"

"She's blaming him for Mai."

"What?"

"Yeah, and now she wants full custody."

We walked into the living room, and Rocko ended the call to pick up Niara. He showered her face with kisses. "My big princess. How are you?"

Her arms were wrapped tightly around his neck. "I'm good. How are you?"

He chuckled. "Daddy's good now."

Troi placed Tajsa down so she could crawl and walk around. Niara immediately started playing with her as soon as Rocko put her down on her feet.

"What's up, Heather?" Rocko asked with a grin. "You growing your hair out?"

"Hey. Yeah, I decided to let it grow some. You look happy."

"I'm happy, other than a little drama I have to deal with."

"Yeah, Troi was filling me in."

"I'm not going to sweat it too hard. I'll work it out. So, what's new since the last time we talked?"

"Nothing much going on other than working and waiting on this law school stuff."

"I'm happy you're pursuing your dreams and shit."

"Thank you. What y'all got planned?" I said.

"We're going to chill at the house. I might throw something on the grill. You should stay for dinner," he replied.

Troi nodded, with a smile.

I was cool with Rocko, and I was even cool with Troi, but there was no way I would have a barbecue with them, like we were one big, happy family. That was where I had to draw the line.

"Thanks for the invite, but I'm going to head back to the city. I gotta work in the morning. I'll be back to get Ni Sunday night."

"I want to keep her for a week, if that's okay with you," Rocko said.

A whole week? What would I do without my baby for an entire week?

"Yeah, I guess so, if you want her that long."

"It's good. Troi and I already discussed it. We could alternate weeks until she starts school."

"So, this means you're going to be staying here with Troi?" I asked.

"Yeah, she finally let a nigga move in. We're getting married."

I had had no idea they were still going to get married. The last time I'd talked to Troi, she had said she wasn't going to marry him. This was good news, though, but a part of me was a little jealous. She would be getting Rocko at his best.

"When is the wedding?" I heard myself ask.

He looked at Troi, so that she would be the one to answer, and she replied, "September."

"September of this year? Like, in a few months?"

Troi nodded. "Yeah."

"Congratulations. I'm really happy for you two."

"Thank you," she answered.

"Thanks," he said.

"Well, I'm going to go ahead and get on the road. Niara, give me a kiss before I leave."

She hugged me. I placed a kiss on her lips. "Bye, Mommy."

"Bye, baby. You be a good girl for Daddy and Miss Troi."

"Okay." She went back to playing with her sister.

I walked out of their home and got into my car. I bit my lower lip as I stared out the window, thinking about what my cousin had said about Dante's baby mama and son. It was time to have a talk with him.

Chapter 37

Dante

"Detective Morgan, a young woman is here to see you," Travis said as he came over to my desk.

I was in the middle of looking over a file, and I wasn't in the mood to be disturbed. What woman wanted to talk to me? It was rare that I was ever at the station, so who would know that I was there?

"Who is it?" I asked, with a deep frown on my face.

"Do you know a Heather Myles?"

My heart skipped a few beats when I heard her name. Heather hadn't returned any of my calls, so I hadn't expected her to show up here, wanting to talk to me.

"All right. Give me a sec."

I closed the folder. My mind was going to a million places as I walked to the front. The first view of her beautiful face had me weak in the knees. I had missed the hell out of her. Her hair had grown to a bob, and it was flattering on her, made her look so mature.

To my surprise, she smiled at me. It was a warm greeting, and my nervousness settled.

I said, "Hey, Heather. What are you doing here?"

"Hi. Um . . . is there somewhere we can go and talk?" she replied.

"You want to talk outside?"

"I was thinking more like talking over some coffee or something. Can you leave right now?"

"There's a Starbucks down the street," I answered. "I can leave anytime I want."

"Okay."

I held the door open for her to walk out. "Is everything okay?" I asked once we were outside.

"Everything is good. Rocko was released this morning. I came down here to drop Niara off to him. I figured that before I went back to San Francisco, I would stop by and see you."

We walked.

"So what brings you here today?" I asked her.

"I can't stop thinking about you."

"Really? Me?"

"Yes, you."

"I thought you hated me for not telling you the truth."

"I was hurt, but I understand you had a job to do. I needed time to figure it all out. I was worried that you used me to bring Rocko down."

"I mean, I don't blame you for thinking that way, because I was working on an investigation, but we wanted someone he used to work with."

"Ah, the infamous Queen."

"You know her?"

"Queen was notorious in our neighborhood, growing up. Everybody knew her. Rocko hasn't done business with her in years."

"Yeah, that was what he said." I changed the subject because I didn't want to talk about Queen or Rocko. "Are you okay? You look great."

"I've been good. I graduated from SF State, with a BA in criminal justice. I'm applying to law school now."

I grinned. "That's an amazing accomplishment. Congratulations."

"Thank you."

I opened the front door to Starbucks for her. The line was a little long, but we stood in it.

"It's always packed up in here," I said.

"No surprise. Most Starbucks are this way. My treat," she said.

"You're buying me coffee? That's nice of you," I replied.

I stared at her as she smiled. I had really missed seeing her. Looking at her made me feel like I never, ever wanted her to leave my sight again.

"What?" she asked.

"Nothing. It's that I'm still in shock that you're standing in front of me."

She nodded as she replied, "It feels strange seeing you in your uniform, but it's actually kind of hot."

I laughed and felt my cheeks get hot. "I know you're not trying to make me blush right now."

"I think I still know how to do that."

"Mm-hmm. You're good at that."

The line moved quicker than expected. We ordered two caramel macchiatos with soy and extra caramel. Before she could pay, I paid for them.

"Hey, I said I was treating you," she complained.

"I know you wanted to, but I can't let you do that. Not today, anyway. I owe you."

She shrugged. "All right. Your loss."

I laughed. "Let's sit right here."

While we waited for our coffee, we sat near a window. For a few seconds, Heather stared at me without saying anything.

"What's on your mind, beautiful?" I questioned.

"Have you heard from your son?"

I hadn't heard from him, and my search seemed like an impossible mission. "Not yet."

"I have a cousin who can find anyone. She found your son's mother."

"She did?"

"Yes, and she spoke with her."

I swallowed the hard lump that started to form in my throat. The look in her eyes told me that she knew the story, but I wondered if that part of my life was something she couldn't handle.

"Dante, did you hear me?"

"Yeah. You said that your cousin found Renee and Naiim. I'm speechless. What did Renee say?"

"She told my cousin about how you met and why she went into hiding. She wants to keep things the way they are."

I nodded, because I knew that. "First, you didn't have to try to get in touch with them for me, but I appreciate you for doing it. To hear that she and Naiim are alive makes me happy. Given the situation, I am okay with her and Naiim staying away. I wish things were different, but it is what it is. It doesn't change my love for my son."

"I understand. I wouldn't have done it if I knew the story. I feel kind of crazy for prying."

"No, it's okay."

"I also came here to talk about something else."

"Okay," I replied.

"If your feelings are truly genuine, like you say they are, then I would like to see where this journey takes us. That's if you're still interested."

"I, too, would like to see where this journey takes us. I don't care about how we met. All I know is that my feelings are real," I said.

She smiled. "That makes me feel so good."

"From this day forward, my plan is to keep you feeling good."

I reached over the table to get a kiss. She met me halfway. As soon as her lips touched mine, I felt tingly all over. We were finally sharing our first kiss, and it felt like fireworks.

Chapter 38

Rocko

Troi and I went to the family courthouse to speak with a family law facilitator. I wasn't going to sit back and let Leslie, Mai's mother, take Junior without a fight. Once we had passed through the large double doors, we found our way to the self-help center's window.

The facilitator there looked up Mai's mother in the computer. Then he said, "She filed for an ex parte hearing to establish guardianship. The judge looked at your criminal record and agreed that you should have supervised visitation when allowed."

I looked over at Troi, and she looked sad for me.

"Is there something I can do to change this?" I asked the facilitator.

"You can file to take her to court or wait to see if your son's grandmother will start supervised visits."

Leslie hated me. I was the reason she was raising her grandson. I tried not to hang my head in defeat, but I felt defeated. I walked away from the self-help center's window, and Troi walked behind me.

"You want to file to take her to court?" Troi asked in a low voice.

"Yeah, I will. Right now I just want to get out of here."

"I'm sorry, babe," she said once we were outside. "You never know what will happen. Give it some time. You can start with supervised visits, and once she sees that you're doing well, she'll change."

"I don't need anyone looking over me while I visit my son. I did that shit enough while in prison." I put on my shades and walked to the car. "Let's go pick up Niara and Tajsa. You feel up to taking them to John's Incredible Pizza?"

"That sounds like fun. I'm sure the girls will love it."

I hopped into the driver's seat. As soon as Troi was in and had her seat belt on, I pulled out of the parking space.

"Have you been looking for a job?" she asked once we were on the road.

"Yeah, but it's been hard. Not many want to hire a felon." I had been looking and applying, but I wasn't getting any callbacks.

"I have this number I want you to call. There's this program that helps parolees."

"Okay, I'll check it out." I reached over and squeezed her hand. I was happy I had her support.

After spending the day with the kids at John's Incredible Pizza, we were exhausted. The kids fell asleep in the car on the way home. Once we got there, we put them right to bed. Then Troi and I got into our pajamas. I poured some red wine, and we cuddled on the couch and watched the latest *Fast & Furious* movie.

My cell phone rang in my pajama pocket.

"Rocko, I thought you said you were going to turn off your phone?" Troi said.

"My bad, babe. Let me see who it is." I pulled out my phone, looked at it, and saw it was a number I didn't recognize. I sent whoever it was to voicemail. A few minutes later, I had a notification that someone had left a message. I had a visual voicemail, so I read the message to myself.

Rocky? It's been a long time since I talked to you. I got your number from your aunt. This is Dominique. I don't know if you remember me or not. I'm sure you do remember me. Well, there's something I really need to talk to you about. Give me a call back as soon as you get this message. Okay. Bye.

I frowned. The only Dominique who called me Rocky was Queen's niece. I used to mess around with her my freshman year of high school. It was strange timing, considering I hadn't been in touch with anyone related to Queen, and I wasn't trying to be in touch. The last thing I needed was to go down for Queen. I stared blankly at Dominique's message, trying to figure out if I would call the number back.

Troi sighed loudly. She never liked our movie time to be interrupted by my phone. When I was out there on the street, my phone never stopped ringing. Watching movies was always impossible.

Wrapping my arms around her, I said, "My bad, babes. I'm turning my phone off."

"Good." She smiled.

It felt good to be wrapped up in her arms. In less than half an hour, Troi had fallen asleep in my arms. I finished the movie without her. I woke her up so we could go upstairs to bed.

"I missed the movie?" she asked wearily.

I turned off the TV. "Yeah. It's all good. We'll finish it some other time."

She yawned. "Yeah."

I checked on the girls before I got into the bed with her.

"Good night," she said.

"Night."

I closed my eyes. Within minutes, I was asleep.

Troi went to work first thing in the morning, and I got the girls up to eat breakfast. While they ate, I called the number Troi had given me for that program to help me find work. The guy wasn't in his office, so I left a message. As soon as I ended the call, the same number Dominique had called from the night before appeared on my screen. I had almost forgotten that she called.

I answered the call. "Hello."

"Is this Rocky?" Dominque asked in her strong Spanish accent.

"Yeah. Dominique?"

"Yeah, it's me."

"This is Queen's niece, right?"

"So, you do remember me?"

"I do. How you been?"

She answered, "I've been good. It's been a long time. You're a hard man to find."

"Why you looking for me?"

"I heard you moved to Sacramento, and then I heard you were doing some time. I ran into your aunt Aleaya at Westfield Mall in the city. She gave me your number."

I scowled. My aunt had always had a big mouth, and my business wasn't any of hers to spread. I was sitting there, trying to figure out why Dominique was trying so hard to find me. I looked over at the girls. Niara was drinking her milk, and Tajsa was throwing what was left of her waffles on the linoleum floor.

"So, what's up?" I asked, hoping it had nothing to do with Queen.

"There's something I have to talk to you about in person."

I didn't know what she wanted to talk about, but there was no way I was going to meet up with an ex–high school fling to talk about anything. It wasn't smart to do, especially not when I was working on my relationship with Troi.

"I don't think that's a good idea. I'm sure we can talk about whatever it is you want to talk about over the phone."

She paused, as if she hadn't expected me to say that. "Okay. I mean, I can talk over the phone, but I really think this is something you want me to say to your face."

"Does this have anything to do with Queen?"

"No, not at all. This is about you and me. When are you free?"

"Look, Dominique, I'm not sure what your angle is, and I'm not sure what my aunt has told you, but I'm engaged and happy in a relationship."

"I know. Do you want me to meet with both of you? I can do that too. This may be something you both need to hear, anyway."

I took the phone away from my ear and scowled at it, as if she could see me. "I need you to cut the fucking bullshit and tell me why you're calling me. I don't have time for games."

"You remember when I got pregnant?"

I closed my eyes, and my heart sped up. "Yeah, but you didn't keep the baby, or at least that was what you told everybody."

"I moved to Oakland Hills to be with my grandmother when my parents caught you in my bedroom."

"Yeah, I remember all of that. You had an abortion, and you moved away."

"That's only half of the truth."

"So, you didn't move to Oakland Hills?" I asked.

"No, I moved to Oakland Hills. I just never got the abortion."

I heard her, but I didn't want to. I grew silent.

"Our son's name is Domiano, and he will be thirteen in a few months."

"Get the fuck out of here. You can't be serious right now."

"I've been trying to find you. When our son was two, I tried to locate you, but you were in jail," she explained.

"When he was two? What about telling me you didn't get the abortion from the jump?"

"I was only fourteen, Rocko."

"I was too. We agreed we were too young to be parents."

"I know, but I couldn't go through with it. By the time I built up the courage to do it, it was too late. He's asking me more questions about you, and I don't want to lie and put this off any longer."

This was splendid fucking news. How was I going to tell Troi this shit? We were finally on good terms, and now I would have to say to her that the girl I got pregnant at fourteen had really kept the baby.

"What's his name again?" I asked.

"Domiano Ramos."

I sighed. The boy didn't even have my last name.

"I don't want to sound like an asshole, Dominique, but, um, I gotta know for sure. I want a test before I go around announcing to the world that we have a son together."

"You really want a test when you know you were my first and only at that time?"

"It's been a really long time, and I'll need the proof for my fiancée."

"Okay. We can have a DNA test done, but I'm pretty sure once she sees him, she'll know."

"You got any pics of him that you can text me in the meantime?"

"I can send a couple. I'll make arrangements for the test too."

"Cool. I gotta go. Let me know when the test is and where, so we can get this over with."

"Will do."

"All right."

"Bye," she said.

I ended the call, and my mind wandered off. I had a twelve-year-old kid, and now I was going to have to tell Troi the news. I picked up the pieces of waffle Tajsa had thrown down.

"Tajsa, you're not supposed to throw the food on the floor. You're supposed to eat it, baby. Niara, if you're done eating, put your plate in the sink and go wash your hands."

"I'm done." She got down from the table and put her plate in the sink.

While I cleaned up Tajsa's hands and mouth, a picture text came through to my phone. I sat down and opened the message. The boy looked like any other mixed kid, but when I stared at the second picture of him, in which he was smiling, a baseball cap on his head and diamond earrings in his ears, I knew he was mine.

I sat in the chair, feeling crazy inside. Troi was going to kill me.

I texted Dominique. Meet me in Sacramento, at the Cheesecake Factory near Arden Fair Mall, around seven thirty tonight. Bring my son with you.

She texted me back right away. Okay. See you then.

Chapter 39

Troi

"What kind of wedding dress do you want?" Erika asked before putting a forkful of chicken Caesar salad in her mouth.

We were having lunch at one of our favorite places, La Bou. We both had ordered salads, a baguette with dill sauce, and some passion fruit iced tea.

"I don't want anything too princess-like or fluffy. I want something sleek and formfitting, kind of mermaidish."

"Oh, yeah. That's going to be hella cute. You did lose your baby weight, plus some."

"Stress will make you lose weight even when you don't want to. I couldn't sleep right while Rocko was away," I confessed.

"I know. It's always hard when they are away from home. I'm happy for you, and even happier that Rocko has matured. You guys have always made a cute couple."

"You know, with all the shit Rocko put me through, I had to think really hard about taking his ass back. He's so different now that he's not in the streets."

"I hope he stays that way. I didn't think dogs could learn new tricks, but I've been wrong before."

"I love my daughter, and I love Rocko. They're everything to me."

"Troi, you don't have to justify shit to me. If you're happy, girl, then I'm happy for you."

"And I *am* happy these days."

"Well, then, that's all that matters."

My mother thought I was crazy for taking Rocko back, but I couldn't make my heart stop beating so hard every time I was around him.

A text message came through from Rocko.

What time you coming home? I have a meeting at seven thirty. Can you keep an eye on Niara for me?

I answered him quickly. Yeah. I'll be home by six. What type of meeting?

"Is that Rocko?" Erika asked.

"Yeah."

"I should've known by the way your face lit all up. This reminds me of how you two used to be back when you first met. Do you still have that feeling?"

"Yeah, it's almost as if we hit the reset button. He's asking me to keep an eye on Niara for him tonight because he has some meeting."

"I know that has to be tough, being the third baby mama. You ever feel weird looking after his other kids?"

"I have my moments, but Niara is a sweetie, and she's so cute. Junior is just as adorable, but his grandmother isn't letting him come around right now. Rocko does good with taking care of what he needs to take care of. Heather and I get along, so that makes it easier. With Mai gone, we don't have any headaches."

"I feel so bad about what happened to her."

"Even though she got on my nerves, she didn't deserve that," I replied.

I looked down at my phone to see if Rocko had answered me. He hadn't. I wanted to know what type of meeting he was having.

I texted him. What kind of meeting, Rocko?

He finally answered me. I'll talk to you about it after the meeting.

I drank my iced tea, hoping he wasn't easing his way back into the street life, which he had promised to leave in the past.

Erika eyeballed me as she asked, "You okay?"

"Yeah. I'm just trying to figure out what Rocko has going on tonight. He was vague, but he said he'll tell me about it later."

"Try to think positively until he tells you."

"Yeah, that's all I can do. Anyway, any new love interests lately?"

"Girl, please. I'm so sick of dating." She laughed, shaking her head.

After work, I grabbed a few things from the grocery store. The girls needed some lunchtime snacks. As soon as I pulled up, Rocko helped me bring the groceries in.

"Hey, babe. How was your day?" he said.

"It was pretty good. How was your day with the girls?"

"Chill. You know how we do. I was trying to get Tajsa to sit on her potty, but, uh, she wasn't having it."

I laughed. "I don't think she's ready yet. I mean, she's only one, Rocko."

"I know, but I wanted to see if she would do it for me. We watched a few movies and took a nap." He placed the bags on the table and glanced at his watch.

It was six thirty.

"You on your way out?" I asked.

"Yeah." He kissed me on the cheek. "It shouldn't take me too long."

I looked at what he was wearing, a black T-shirt, blue jeans, and black Jordans. He was freshly shaved and lined up. His cologne smelled delicious. "Hmm, where's this meeting?"

He answered, "At a restaurant. I'll fill you in as soon as I get back."

I sighed and looked at the girls, who were playing on the living-room floor. Something wasn't right.

Chapter 40

Rocko

I was standing in front of the Cheesecake Factory when Dominique valet parked her red Lexus ES 350. Domiano walked slightly behind her as they approached me. They both were wearing designer brands. At least she kept him up, I thought to myself. The closer they got, the more I could see that Domiano even walked like me.

I looked at her. Dominique's hair and makeup were flawless. Her small waist, hips, full breasts, and legs were on point. I shifted my eyes away quickly.

"Hey, Nique," I said.

Her eyes lit up as she replied, "I thought that was you, but I wasn't sure. Your goatee makes you look so different. I like it. I want you to meet your son, Domiano. Domiano, this is Rocko . . . your father."

Domiano stared at me without a smile. I couldn't figure out what he was thinking as he observed everything I was wearing.

"Nice to meet you, Domiano," I said.

Domiano lowered his eyes as he replied, "Nice to meet you too."

I said, "Let's go inside and talk."

I opened the door for them, and they entered the restaurant. I followed them inside and told the hostess that we needed a table for three. She sat us near the back of the place, by a window.

"I love the Cheesecake Factory," Dominique said as soon as we were seated.

I noticed a giant engagement ring on her finger as she moved her hair over her shoulder.

"I see you're getting married too," I said.

"Oh, no," she said. "It's a gift from a friend. We're not engaged."

"Pretty expensive nonengagement gift."

"This is nothing." She looked at the menu. "Now that you see Dom, you still want a paternity test?"

"Yeah. Like I said, it's for my fiancée. How soon can we get one?"

"Well, we live in Las Vegas. I'm out here for only a few days. I would like to get it before I leave."

"When did you move to Las Vegas?" I asked.

"When my grandmother died after I graduated from high school, I moved there with a boyfriend. That's where we've been ever since."

I nodded.

A waitress came to the table. "Hello. I'm your server for the evening. Can I get you something to drink?"

"Lemonade," Domiano and I said at the same time.

I smiled at him, but he didn't smile back.

"I'll take a margarita," Dominique added.

"I'll be right back with two lemonades and a margarita."

The waitress left the three of us to look over the menu. Every time I looked up, Dom was staring at me with curiosity. Every time we locked eyes, he would lower his.

"Would you like for me to call you Domiano or Dom?" I asked him.

"I'm cool with Dom."

"All right. When will you be thirteen?"

"October ninth."

I raised my eyebrows. "My birthday is October tenth."

He replied, "I know."

I stared at Dominique. "He was born a day before my birthday, and you still didn't think to tell me?"

"My parents were crazy, Rocky. Don't you remember? I had no way to tell you."

"But I didn't even hear rumors that you kept him."

"I didn't see anyone while I was pregnant. I was with my grandmother in Oakland Hills. My cousins didn't even know until he was almost a year old."

I hummed. "I see. What type of work do you do in Vegas?"

I wondered if she had been in the family business or had a legit hustle to afford the luxury things she had.

She laughed a little. "Oh no, Rocky. I don't work."

"You don't? How do you support yourself?" I was curious to see if she would mention anything about her aunt.

"You know my family. We want for nothing."

"You work with Queen?" I asked, raising my eyebrow.

"Tía Dadiana is a very special woman. She taught me everything I know," Dominique replied. "Why you ask?"

"Does she know about our reunion?"

"No. I did this on my own for Dom. He's been wanting to meet you for some time."

"I see." I dropped the subject of Queen because I didn't want Dominique to think I had a problem with her. "You guys ready to order food?"

"I am. What about you, Dom?"

"I'm ready," he replied.

I didn't stay at the Cheesecake Factory for long after we finished eating dinner. I brought Troi a piece of her favorite classic strawberry cheesecake and put it in the refrigerator.

I went upstairs and checked on the girls. They were asleep. I headed into the bedroom, and just then, Troi came out of the bathroom, wrapped in a towel. The top half of her body and her hair were dripping wet. She looked surprised to see me.

"You scared me. You're back so fast," she said.

"Told you it wouldn't take long."

I changed out of my clothes and put on some basket-ball shorts.

"So, are you going to tell me what kind of meeting it was?"

I swallowed hard. "Of course, I am." My first thought was to lie, but I had done that enough in the past. Lying had never worked, and if I lied, Troi would hand me my ass. "Put on your pajamas and dry your hair first. When you come to bed, I'll tell you."

I needed more time to gather my thoughts.

The deep scowl on her face spelled out worry, but she went ahead and got into her gown. The whole time while she blow-dried her hair, I was trying to figure out a good way to be honest.

After she was done, she stood in the bathroom door-way and watched me pace. "Okay, now you're scaring me."

"Can you sit down on the bed or on that chair?" I asked her.

She folded her arms across her chest. "I don't want to sit down, because something is telling me that what you have to say isn't good news."

I sat down on the chair and said, "Troi, I got a call last night, when we were watching that movie. A woman from my past named Dominique left me a voice message, telling me that she needed to talk to me and—"

"Who the fuck is Dominique?"

"Will you let me tell you?"

She blew air from her lips, while her eyes became intense. "Go ahead. Finish."

"So, like I was saying . . . Dominique said she had some-thing important to tell me. I hit her back this morning, and she told me that she has a twelve-year-old son."

"What does her son have to do with you?"

"She said he's mine."

Troi laughed. "You're kidding, right?"

"I wish I was kidding."

"So, you were, like, what, fourteen when you got her pregnant?"

"Yeah, but I didn't know she had the baby. She told me her parents were making her get an abortion. When she moved away, I never checked back with her. So, I met up with her and the little boy at the Cheesecake Factory tonight. I had to see him in person."

"And you couldn't tell me that before you went?"

"I wanted to, but I had to see if he looked anything like me first."

"You could've told me last night, when she called, and we could've gone to see them together."

"I thought about that, but I had to see to make sure before involving you. I know how you get down. You probably would've tried to fight her."

She thought about it before she asked, "Do you think he looks like you?"

"To me, he's almost a spitting image, but I still want a DNA test to be sure."

"What's his name?"

"Domiano Ramos."

"She didn't give him your last name?"

"Nope. He has her last name."

"You got a picture of him?"

I pulled my phone out of my jeans and brought up his picture. I stood up and handed her my phone.

She gasped at first sight. "He's your twin."

"You think so?"

She nodded slowly. "Yup. How you feeling about all of this?"

"I'm pissed because I felt like she could've told me a long time ago, but she claims her parents didn't want her to have anything to do with me."

Troi didn't appear to be angry as she continued to stare at the boy's picture. "Rocko, your genes are strong as fuck. I'm sure you see what I see."

"Yeah, but I still need that test, don't you think?"

"Yeah, get the test. Thank you, baby, for telling me. I appreciate that."

"I had to tell you, babes. We're going to be married, and I can't walk around here holding secrets anymore. I learned my lesson the hard way. I can't do anything to risk losing you ever again."

She handed me back my phone.

"I know you were young, and you've made quite a few mistakes, but, nigga, don't you believe in condoms?"

I sighed as I said, "I swear, it doesn't seem like it, but I've used plenty of condoms."

"I can't tell." She shook her head at me. "Well, it is what it is. I hope you know I'm not having any more kids. You having four before you're thirty is crazy to me."

"So, you don't want to have another one by me?" I frowned.

"Good night, Rocko." She waved her hand at me.

"Good night, babes."

Chapter 41

Troi

I went with Rocko to his paternity test because he wanted me to go with him. When I got a first glance at Dominique, I wasn't surprised at her beauty, because that was how Rocko rolled, but then I felt a little self-conscious. I mean, this bitch was dressed in everything brand name from head to toe. She wore them Christian Louboutins as if those shoes were made exclusively for her feet.

Rocko introduced us. "Dominique, this is my fiancée, Troi. Troi, this is Dominique, Domiano's mother."

"It's nice to meet you," Dominique said.

I shook her hand. "Wow, you have a handsome kid."

"Thank you," she replied. "Domiano, are you gonna say hello?"

The boy didn't speak, not even when Rocko said what's up to him. He kept his eyes on his Nintendo Switch.

We sat in the waiting room until the nurse was ready for them. When their names were called, Rocko and Domiano went into the back room to be swabbed. It was over with quickly. The nurse said the results would be back within three to ten business days. The office would send the results via mail to them.

"I'm going to head back to Vegas tonight," Dominique said to Rocko as we all stood in the waiting room. "Once the results come in, give me a call. I don't have time to check my mail all the time. I might miss it."

Rocko nodded. "I'll call you."

She winked at him and then sauntered through the door, with her son following behind her. He didn't even say goodbye. What the hell was in her eye? Why was she swishing so hard?

As we left the office, I looked over at Rocko to see if he was looking at her ass. He wasn't.

Rocko glanced over at me and stared, as if to say, "Don't start any shit."

"What?" I asked.

"You're funny," he replied.

"How am I funny?"

"You were frowning at her the whole time. Babes, I'm your man, and I know you. I'm not trying to hit that."

"I know you aren't, but I don't trust her," I said as we reached the parking lot.

He chuckled and started walking toward the car. I followed behind him. Before I reached the car, I looked over to the left and noticed Dominique sitting in her car, staring right at us. What the fuck was that bitch staring at?

Rocko opened the door for me to get in the car. Once he was in the driver's seat, I asked, "Are you hoping Domiano isn't your son?"

"I'm not hoping for anything. I mean, if he's mine, then he's mine. If he's not, then he's not. In any case, I'm prepared for the outcome."

"I hear you. If he's your son, then you'll have to try to bond with him."

"Definitely. He's distant, but that will change with time."

"What are you going to do about her wanting to fuck you?"

He laughed at me. "She doesn't want to fuck me."

"You must be blind or pretending like you're blind."

"Troi, are you going to start acting insecure on me again?"

"If I'm acting insecure, it's because you made me this way."

Rocko sighed loudly. "I know I fucked up in the past. But it's a new day, and I thought we were over that bullshit. Dominique is nothing for you to worry about. Trust me."

I rolled my eyes at him. "Yeah, okay."

I had seen the lust in that bitch's eyes. She wanted Rocko.

When I looked at Rocko, he seemed sincere. I wanted to relax, but I knew deep down that this would be a test for him to see if he was strong enough to resist that temptation.

Chapter 42

Rocko

Domiano was 99.8 percent my kid. I laid the letter down and stared at Troi.

"Well, what does it say?" she asked.

"He's mine."

She exhaled and nodded her head. "What now?"

"I'm going to call Dominique to see if she got hers, and then I have to start spending time with my son."

Troi didn't say another word as she walked out the front door. She needed some space, and I respected that. As much as she had said she could handle the results, the news still stung like a bee.

I called Dominique, and she answered right away. "Hey, Rocko."

"Dominique, I got the results back. Did you get yours?"

"I haven't checked the mail. What does it say?"

"He's mine."

"Well, I knew that. I'm glad you know for sure."

"Is he at school right now?" I asked.

"Yeah, he's at school. As soon as he gets home, I'll tell him the news. He's going to be happy."

"You think so? He's barely said two words to me since I met him."

"That's because he was afraid that you wouldn't be his father. He'll be happy for sure."

"Okay, good. I'll be coming down to Vegas to see him soon, or you may have to bring him to me."

"He would like that very much . . . and I would like that too."

"All right. Well, I'll talk to you later."

"Bye."

I ended the call and sat on the couch. The news made me think about my baby son, Junior. I needed to see him again, so I called Mai's mother, but she didn't answer. I left a message.

"Hey, Leslie. This is Rocko. I miss my son. Can I arrange something with you to see him? Let me know."

As soon as I hung up, a text message from Dominique came through. It was a picture of her naked. *Fuck!* Flesh. Nipples. A sexy, sly grin. *Shit!* She looked even better naked than she did with clothes on. I sighed, erased the picture, and didn't respond to the text. She obviously wanted some attention. She wasn't going to get it from me.

My cell started ringing. I thought I would have to cuss Dominique out, but it wasn't her.

"Hello."

"Rocko?"

I sat straight up. I recognized that voice instantly.

"Queen?" I asked.

"The one and only," she responded. "How's my favorite guy?"

When did I become her favorite guy?

"I'm cool. How you been?"

"I'm alive. I heard about Cipher and Jared, so I was calling to check on you."

"I'm cool. What's up?"

"My niece tells me that you were asking her some questions. You looking for work?"

"Nah. I was asking her if she was in the family business, but I wasn't asking because I want to get back in. Your trail is hot, Queen. The police been asking a whole lot of questions. They tried to hem me up, but I didn't go out like that."

"You think I don't know that. You and I are good. You sure you don't want to work for me?"

"I'm out the game."

"My business hasn't been the same without you."

"I'm trying to keep my hands clean."

"I'm sure those clean hands need money."

"I'm out."

"Okay, but if you change your mind, you know how to find me. Take care."

I ended the call. I exhaled and felt good about my decision. I meant what I had said. I was done with the street hustling.

Chapter 43

Dominique

I was glad the truth was out, and my son could finally have a connection with his real father. For too many years, I had tried to make my life have some sort of normality. Without my strict parents and grandmother to control my life, I had learned how to survive as a single mother and an adult. Having a baby so young hadn't been easy. I had barely finished high school on time, and trying to raise a boy to be a man was getting harder by the day. Rocko was coming back into our lives at the perfect time. Domiano needed him. I *needed* him.

After I hit SEND on the naked pic, I waited for Rocko to respond. He didn't. Was he that faithful to his woman that he wouldn't acknowledge me? My iPhone told me he had looked at the photo. I had heard about Rocko's other baby mothers and how he moved in the street. Why was he dodging me?

I washed my hair and wrapped it in a towel. I waited for Domiano to come home from school, so I could tell him the news.

He walked in with his Beats by Dre headphones covering his ears. I was sure his music was too loud. He tossed his backpack on the couch and flopped down next to me. I motioned for him to take off the headphones.

"Hey, Ma."

"Hey. The test results came back."

"Yeah?"

"Yup. Rocky is your father."

He smiled a little. "I look a lot like him."

"Yes, you do."

"So, what happens now? Do I change my last name to Cooper?"

"If you want to change your last name to Cooper, you can, but what's wrong with Ramos?"

"Ramos is your last name. I want my father's last name."

I held my hands up. "That's fine with me. I'll get started on that ASAP."

"Good." He took a deep breath and exhaled.

"You feel better?"

"Yeah. Feels good to know the truth."

"You're such a smart kid. You have homework?"

He nodded. "A little bit."

"Well, you better get started on it. I'm going out tonight with a few friends."

He rolled his eyes a little. He didn't like me going out every night, but I had nothing else to do with my spare time. I was a stay-at-home mom. The nightlife in Vegas was the only thing that kept me sane. Plus, it put extra cash in my pocket.

While Domiano picked up his backpack and went into his bedroom, a text message came back from Rocko.

Don't do that again.

I smiled as I texted him back. You must want to see me in person. No need to be shy, Rocky.

Rocko texted me right away. Cut it out.

I smirked and tossed my phone on the counter. He was playing hard to get, which was interesting.

Chapter 44

Troi

"I love this dress," I said to Erika.

"That's the one. Say yes to this dress, damn it!"

She was tired of looking at wedding dresses, and so was I, but I wasn't going to stop looking until I found the perfect one. This was the perfect one, so our search was over.

"Yes to this dress," I shouted.

We laughed together. Then Erika looked at the price tag, which was hanging on the side, underneath my arm.

"Girl, do you see how much this dress is?" Her eyes nearly popped out of her head.

"No. How much is it?"

"Almost five thousand dollars."

"What?" I nearly choked on my own saliva.

"How you going to afford it? Rocko not selling dope no more."

I bit my lower lip and shrugged. Rocko had used most of his savings for court fees and lawyer's fees. "I don't know. We'll have to keep looking, then."

Erika whined, "Okay, but this is the one. Wait. They're having a bridal expo soon."

"I'm supposed to be getting married before that comes around. Shit, I'll try to find something like it. Now that I know what I'm looking for, maybe it'll be easier."

I slid into the dressing room to remove the dress. I felt like crying, because I really wanted this dress. If Rocko was still hustling, I would be able to get it. I needed to rearrange my mind so that I thought like a woman on a serious budget. We had a child now. I couldn't go around tossing money like I used to. As soon as I was dressed, I handed the lady back the dress, and we walked out of the store empty handed.

"Five racks on a dress is crazy," Erika said.

"Not when you got it like that. The dress was perfect."

"And it looked perfect on you."

"You're not making it any better, so shut up, Erika."

She laughed. "Okay . . . okay. You hungry?"

"Kind of, but I want to get home to Rocko. He's been in the house, looking after Tajsa for me. So, I'm thinking about taking the rest of the day off."

"Okay. He's been the good stay-at-home daddy lately. I think it's cute."

"Yeah? I think so too."

Instead of going back to work after wedding-dress shopping, I decided to go home a little early. When I got there, Rocko's Range was parked in the driveway. I smiled to myself. I was glad he wasn't out running around. I wanted to surprise him.

"Rocko?" I called once I was inside.

He didn't answer, but he didn't have to. As soon as I entered the living room, I saw him. He was counting his money.

"Hey, babe. What you up to?" I called.

"Hey, babe. Shit. Counting what's left of my money. It's getting low."

"Where's Tajsa?"

"My mom came to get her, so they could go get some ice cream earlier."

I eyed the money, thinking about the dress. "Are you still looking for a job?"

"Yeah, the guy called me back finally. He wants me to come down in the morning. He's interested in my welding certificate. He has something for me at a refinery in West Sac."

"That's great, babe. I'm happy to hear that. You excited?"

"Hell yeah. I was starting to feel like I would never get a job."

"How much they pay?" I asked.

"Starting at twenty-two an hour."

"Not bad."

"I know, right?"

I looked at his money again. "How much you got there?"

He blew air from his lips and replied, "Only ten thousand. I'm going to throw it in the safe. We could use it for the wedding. Just let me know if you need anything."

"I'm glad you said that, because I need about five thousand dollars."

"What you need it for?"

"My wedding dress."

He took half of it and gave it to me. "Here." He placed a sweet kiss on my lips. "I know you're going to look sexy as hell. I can't wait."

I stood there with the money in my hand while Rocko disappeared upstairs. He didn't seem to care that I had asked for half of the little money he had left. That meant a lot to me.

Chapter 45

Dominique

For years I had dreamed of reuniting with Rocko. This was supposed to be my chance. He wasn't married yet, so this was supposed to go my way. Back in the day, it seemed like everyone had stood in our way, especially Heather. I believed that if my parents hadn't stopped me from being with him, Heather wouldn't have stood a chance against me. He would've never been with her, and she would've never had his baby. My parents had had other plans for my life. Being a teenage mother had been hard for me, and even harder without Rocko's help, but my parents had provided for us, and they had made sure we never went without.

I had blamed my family for years for keeping me away from Rocko, but I blamed myself for waiting so long to find the courage to tell him the truth about his son. I was his very first baby mama, and I was here to stay. I felt as if I should've automatically had priority status, but things weren't going exactly the way I had hoped they would. He wasn't even allowing me the opportunity to let him know that I was still in love with him, so my plan to show him my best assets was becoming a waste of my precious time.

Instead of my dropping Domiano off at Troi and Rocko's place for the weekend, Rocko thought it would be a better idea for me to meet up with him at the Chevron gas station. It was close to his house, but he wasn't going to allow me over there. He was acting like it wasn't cool for me to drop my son off over there. I caught an attitude because he was treating me like a damned stalker.

I had sent him a few naked pics, but that was it. When he hadn't gone for my little naked tricks, I'd stopped. He had put Troi on a higher pedestal, even higher than the one he used to put Heather on.

When I got to the Chevron, Rocko was already there, so I pulled up alongside him.

"Go with your dad, *hijo*. I'm gonna get something to drink out of the store."

Domiano gave me a slight head nod. "You going back to Las Vegas tomorrow?"

"No. I'll be at the Hyatt for the whole weekend, until it's time to drive you back home." I studied his face, and his eyebrows were turned downward, and his nose was scrunched up a little bit. He seemed bothered suddenly. "What's the matter, Dom?"

"I don't really know this dude all like that."

"I know, but, Dom, he's your dad. You'll be fine. It's time that you get to know him." I leaned over and kissed him on the side of his handsome face. I loved my son so much, and I truly treasured everything about him.

He opened his car door to get out. I got out with my purse and keys in hand. Rocko eased out of his car and placed his hands in his jeans pockets.

"Hey," he said. "How are you, Dominique?"

I rolled my eyes and walked into the quickie mart. I was throwing my attitude around and didn't care, because I didn't appreciate him treating me like shit and then trying to act like everything was cool. As I walked around the little store, my heels were clicking. My ass swished as I headed to the back, where the drinks were.

Rocko entered the store and made his way over to where I was standing. I was searching for an AriZona Cherry Lime Rickey.

"Is there anything I need to know, like if he's allergic to anything?" Rocko asked.

"Your son isn't a baby, Rocko. He can tell you if he's allergic to anything."

"True." He lingered and grabbed a Pepsi as I quickly walked to the front of the store. He followed me. "He just told me he likes Pepsi."

I turned around to stop him in his tracks. "Yeah, he loves Pepsi."

There was this awkward silence between us. Rocko was staring at me.

"What?" I snarled, my upper lip curling.

"Damn! Is it like that? You big mad, huh?"

"This is how you want it, right? Pick up your son. Drop off your son in a public place, with little to no interaction, right?"

"Nah, I didn't say that. I want you to respect my relationship with Troi, that's all. I didn't say we couldn't talk at all."

"You wouldn't even let me drop Dom off at your house tonight, and now you're acting like I'm supposed to be all buddy-buddy and shit."

"Chill. Troi is uncomfortable right now. Give her some time. She'll come around."

I sucked my teeth and sighed. "So, what are you gonna do about the times you come to Las Vegas to see him? I can't be driving back and forth and taking flights out to Sacramento every time you want me to."

"Next visitation, I'll come out to Vegas, and I'll hit you up about a meeting spot. We don't have to meet at your house. But let's not think about that right now. We'll cross that bridge when the time comes."

I rolled my eyes, turned, and put my drink on the counter. As the guy rang up my drink, I noticed Rocko was still standing behind me, with some distance between us. He was working my last nerve. I continued to ignore his weird body language until I had paid. Then I grabbed my drink, walked out of the store, hopped into my car, waved at my son, and drove off.

Chapter 46

Heather

I felt like I was floating among the clouds as I made my way out of Dante's master bathroom. I had taken a bubble bath, which he had run for me as soon as I had arrived at his house. I'd come over once I dropped off Niara with Rocko.

"Did you tell your mom that we're taking her to lunch tomorrow?" Dante asked.

"I sure did. You know, she asked me when we're moving in together."

"Really? I'm beginning to wonder the same thing. I mean, I'm not rushing you or anything. I'm starting to hate when we have to say goodbye."

This was my first time hearing that he wanted me to move in with him, but I wasn't going to live in Sacramento and commute all the way to San Francisco to go to school. That was crazy to me.

"I need to get through law school."

"They have online classes, don't they? You can commute."

"I'm not going to commute. I don't like driving that much. Plus, my little bucket really isn't fit for driving back and forth."

"You want me to get you a new car?" He raised his eyebrow at me.

I shook my head quickly. I wasn't going to let a man buy me anything, so he could hold it over my head or take it back if things didn't work out between us.

"No, thank you. I'm not doing the commute."

He palmed my ass and then said, "Let me get you something nice. You study hard, and you're fulfilling your dream. Truthfully, I want to do more than buy you a car. I want you and Niara to move in with me. I want to take care of the two of you. You deserve to have everything your heart desires." Dante didn't bite his tongue when he proceeded to ask, "When do you think you'll be ready to have a baby, Heather?"

"Baby? I don't think about having another baby. Besides, I thought marriage came before all that."

"It can if you want it to."

"I don't see you dropping down on your knee and proposing."

To my surprise, he got down on one knee and asked, "Will you marry me, Heather?"

I frowned. "You can't do it like that. Where's the ring at?"

He paused before biting his lower lip. He smiled, as if a naughty thought had crossed his mind. "Look in that top drawer."

My heart started racing. I was simply calling his bluff, but this had been his plan all along. I clutched the towel around my naked body tighter as I opened the top drawer of his dresser. A square black suede box was sitting on top of his folded-up boxers. I took it out, and it seemed as if my breath was trapped in my throat when I realized he really wasn't playing with me.

"Oh, my God," I said.

"Open it."

When I opened the little box, a nice princess-cut diamond ring stared me in the face. It was so stunning and shiny. I was breathless and felt like I didn't know what to do or say. I wasn't ready for marriage. That part I was sure of. I was still trying to get my education in order. I had my own goals I was trying to fulfill.

"Wow," was all I could say.

"Is that a yes or a no?"

"Wow." I kept blinking at it.

"Heather? Is that a yes or a no?"

"I don't know what to say."

Dante was and had been the man that every girl wanted and wished for.

Disappointment filled his eyes. He wanted me more than anything. He didn't have any financial worries, and I didn't want Niara and me to be a financial burden. I was holding back because our lives would change tremendously. I would have to incorporate being a wife, and everything else he wanted me to be, into my current life as a mother and a student. What if I couldn't keep him satisfied? What if he left me and I was a single mother again, the way my father had left my mother? Dante wasn't that type of man, but nothing in life was guaranteed. The thought of having my heart broken again jarred me.

"Will you at least consider it?" he asked. "I don't want to waste my time on another meaningless relationship. I know what I want, and I want to marry you. I love you."

"I love you too, but—"

"I know. It's too much for you right now. I have no problem with you finishing law school and becoming a lawyer. I'm not going to pressure you."

I closed my eyes. I needed to get over my fear. I needed for once to be happy with a man that was for real. This was my time. What the hell? I loved this man, and I couldn't see myself with anyone else.

"Yes," I heard myself say. "I'll marry you."

"Not if you don't mean it."

"I mean it."

I was visibly shaking. He took the box from my shaking hands, with a broad smile on his face, and glided the ring onto my finger. It was a little loose.

"I'll get it sized before the weekend is up," he assured me.

Then he swept me up off my feet and into his arms.

My heart felt like it was going to jump out of my chest.

Chapter 47

Rocko

"You can't see me in *Madden*," Domiano declared after he whupped my ass for the second time in a row.

The boy was a natural shit talker. Yeah, he was my kid.

I tossed the Xbox controller on the couch and said, "You right about that. Shit, after the third touchdown, I knew it was a wrap. I gotta step my *Madden* game up."

I handed him a hundred dollars as I took a bite of pizza.

Niara, Tajsa, and Troi were upstairs watching Princess Tiana, so we had the living room to ourselves.

Domiano's eyes got so big. "*Dang*, you ballin' or something?"

I laughed at him. "No, not anymore. I got a job this morning." To see my son's eyes light up like a Christmas tree in a dark room made me feel good. "You keep those grades up, and you'll see more of that. Your mama keeps you in all the latest shit, so I gotta keep up."

"What kind of work you do?"

"I'm going to be working on fixing holes in metal at a refinery starting next week."

"So, you got a regular job?"

"Yes, indeed. What you want to be when you grow up?"

"I don't know." He shrugged. "I want to go to college."

"You think about going to college?" I asked him.

"Yeah. My mother talks a lot about the family business, but I'm cool."

"What you know about the family business?"

"Everything. I grew up around it my whole life. It's dangerous, and I don't think I would like prison."

I nodded my head, with a smile. "Good kid. I like the way you think. You speak Spanish like your mother?"

"Nah, but I understand it. I asked my mom if I could change my last name to Cooper."

"Oh, yeah? What she say?"

"She's cool with it."

"You're a Cooper, so you should be a Cooper," I declared.

He nodded and looked proud. That made me feel proud. I had missed out on much of his life, but I was happy I would be there for him as he entered his teen years. Those were vital years for a young man.

My cell phone rang just then. I pulled it out of my pocket, looked down at the screen, and saw that it was Mai's mother calling.

I answered quickly. "Hello."

"Rocko?"

"Yeah. Leslie? How are you?"

"I'm good, but this isn't Leslie. This is her sister, Tangie."

"Oh. Hey, Tangie. Is everything all right?"

"Leslie is at the hospital right now, and she would lose her mind if she knew I was calling you from her cell phone, but you're the boy's father, so you should know."

"I should know what? Is everything all right? Where's Junior?"

"He's with me. He's been with me for about a month now. Leslie has stage three breast cancer. It's overly aggressive, and she's extremely sick, going through chemo and all. I wanted to let you know 'cause I don't have the energy to keep up with my great-nephew. Now, my sister begged me not to call you. I have no other choice, though.

I love my baby nephew. I do, but he is a handful. He's walking and getting into every damn thing. I'm too old to raise a baby."

"I understand. I'm fully capable of taking care of my son. If you want, I can get him right now."

"Well, he's sleeping now, but I'll have him ready in the morning."

"What about the legal documents? I don't want Leslie calling the police or anything like that. I'm sure if she pulls through and gets out of the hospital, she'll try to scream kidnapping or something crazy."

"She won't have the strength or the energy. She was trying to sign him over to me, but a boy needs to be with his father. I'll make sure the paperwork is done, okay? I'll call you in the morning with my address."

"Thank you so much for giving me a call, Tangie. I appreciate it."

"No problem. My husband and I don't blame you for what happened to my niece. Tragedies happen in life. It's not fair to keep your baby away from you because of it."

"Thank you again."

"You're welcome. Have a good night, and I'll see you soon."

"You have a good night too."

I hung up the phone and felt sad that Leslie was battling cancer. She had lost her daughter and had had to bury her, and now she was sick herself. I said a silent prayer for her.

Domiano gulped his Pepsi.

"Hey, I got good news. You get to meet your baby brother tomorrow," I told him.

"Cool. How old is he?"

"He's two."

"My mom says you got a bunch of kids."

I laughed. "Something like that."

***

My mother wanted everyone, including Pop, at her house for brunch after I picked up Junior. He had gotten so big, and he looked just like Mai. Mama hugged and kissed him tight because she had missed him so much. She hugged the girls next and placed kisses on their cheeks. Domiano was next in line.

"Dom, this is my mother, your grandmother," I said, making the introduction.

"Hi," he said, with a wide smile on his face.

Mama embraced him. "My goodness, you're so handsome. Look at you."

"It's nice to meet you," he said.

"It's nice to meet you as well, baby. Come in and make yourself comfortable."

"Hey, Mama," Troi said and kissed her next.

"Hey, Troi. Wash your hands so you can help me get this brunch served."

"Okay."

"Hey, Pop," I said as I entered the living room, Domiano right behind me.

He stood from the couch, and we hugged. "Hey, son. The clan is all here."

"Yes, indeed. This is Domiano, your oldest grandson."

"Hey, man," Pop said and extended his arms for a hug. Domiano hugged him.

"Just call me Pop. That's what everyone calls me."

"Okay," Domiano answered.

I sat on the couch next to Pop, and Dom sat next to me. Junior had taken to Dom fast. He wanted Dom to pick him up, so he did. Niara chased Tajsa around the couch.

I couldn't do anything but thank God for the things He was doing in my life. I had a job, I was marrying the woman of my dreams, and I had all my children with me.